Toots and Doodles...Scanned and....Busted!

by
Shawna Lynn Lewellen

To: Lucy

Enjoy!! :)

SHAWNA LEWELLEN

Published by Shawna Lewellen

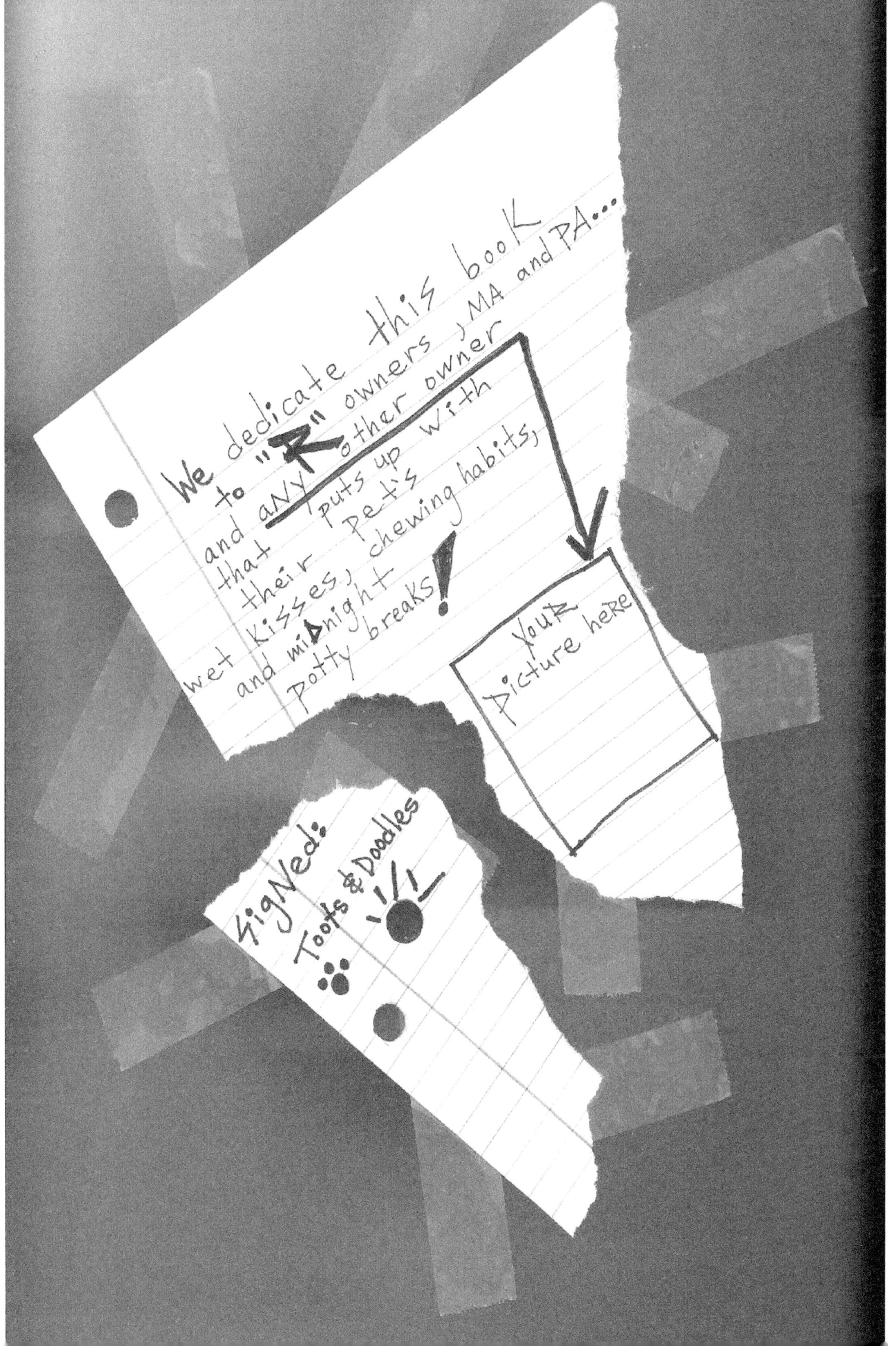
We dedicate this book
to "R" owners, MA and PA...
and aNY other owner
that puts up with
their pet's
wet Kisses, chewing habits,
and miDnight
potty breaks!
YOUR picture here
SigNed: Toots & Doodles

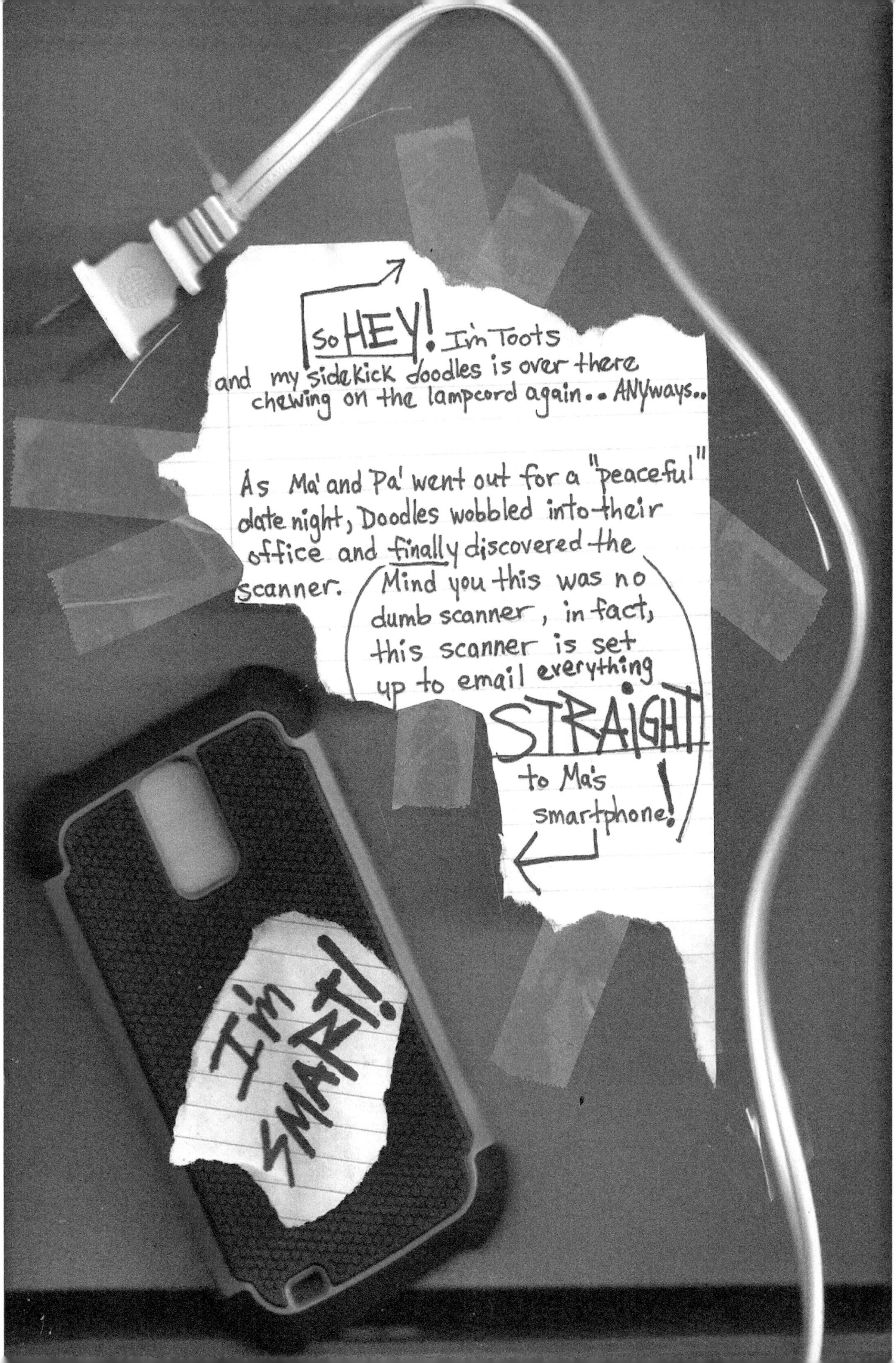
So HEY! I'm Toots
and my sidekick doodles is over there chewing on the lampcord again.. ANYways..
As Ma' and Pa' went out for a "peaceful" date night, Doodles wobbled into their office and finally discovered the scanner.
Mind you this was no dumb scanner, in fact, this scanner is set up to email everything STRAIGHT to Ma's smartphone!
I'm SMART!

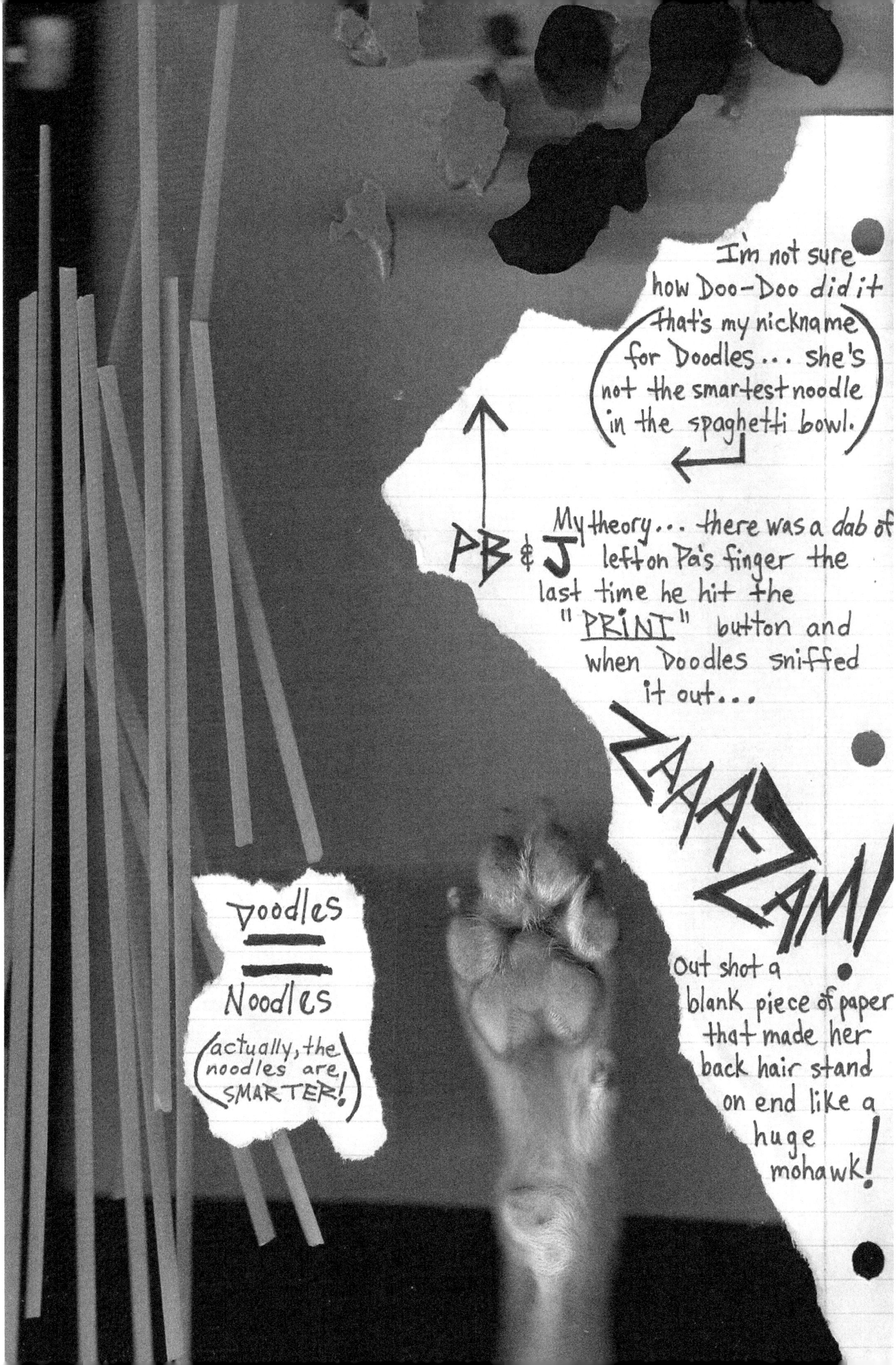

I'm not sure how Doo-Doo did it
(that's my nickname for Doodles... she's not the smartest noodle in the spaghetti bowl.)
PB & J
My theory... there was a dab of PB & J left on Pa's finger the last time he hit the "PRINT" button and when Doodles sniffed it out...
ZAAA-ZAM!
Out shot a blank piece of paper that made her back hair stand on end like a huge mohawk!
Doodles
=
Noodles
(actually, the noodles are SMARTER!)

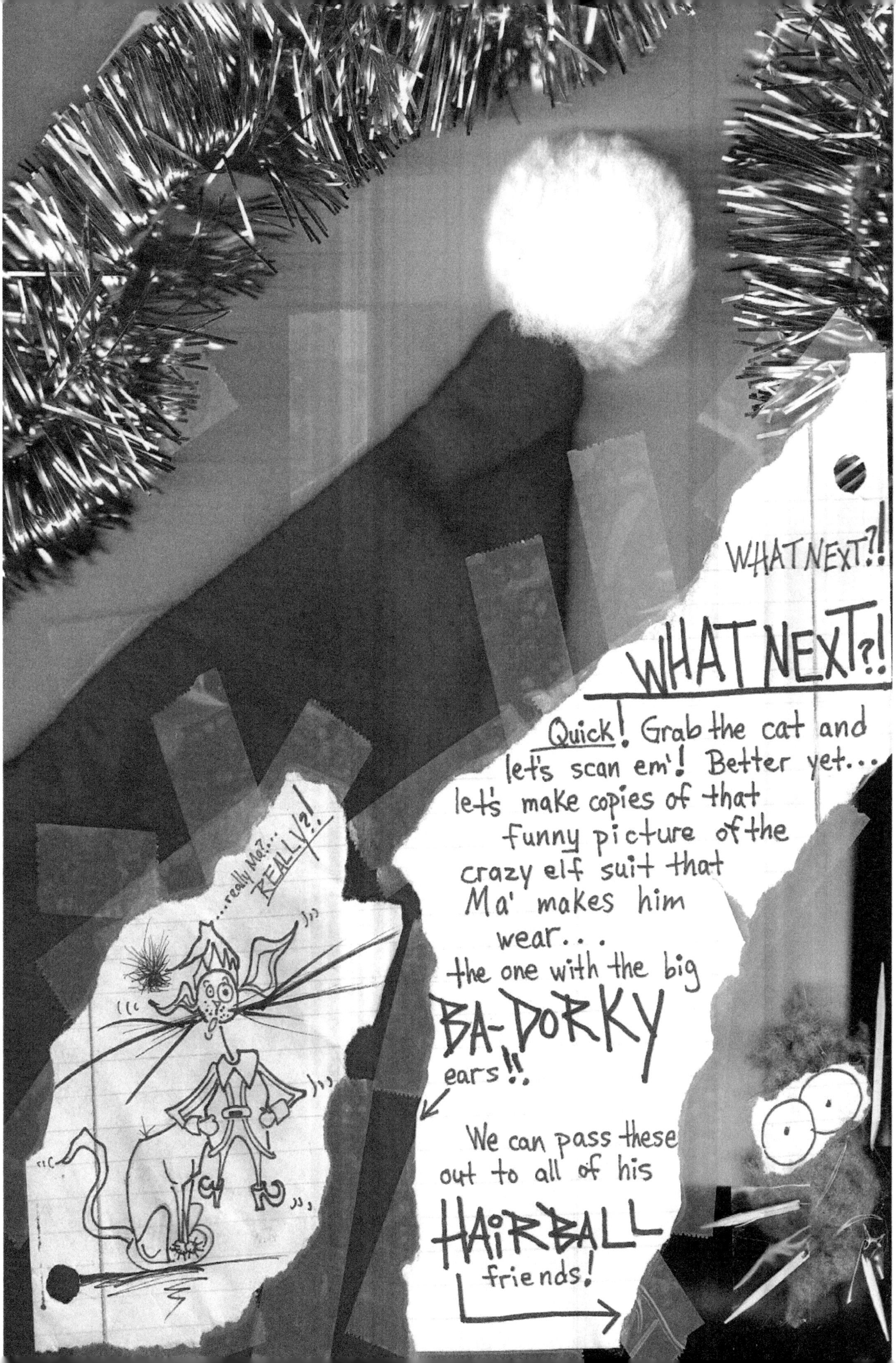

WHAT NEXT?!
WHAT NEXT?!
Quick! Grab the cat and let's scan em'! Better yet... let's make copies of that funny picture of the crazy elf suit that Ma' makes him wear... the one with the big BA-DORKY ears!!
...really Ma?... REALLY?!
We can pass these out to all of his HAIRBALL friends!

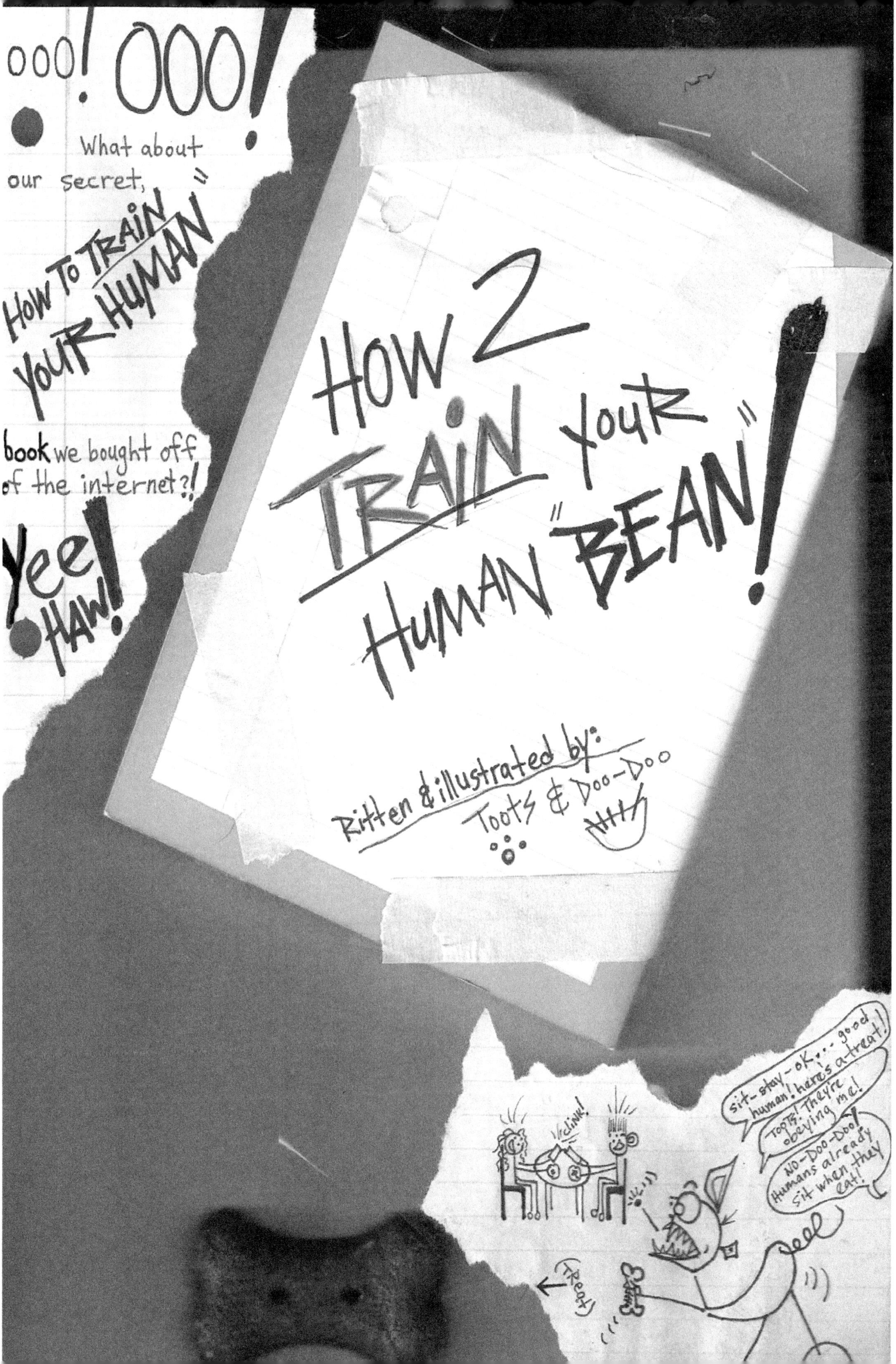
ooo! OOO!
What about our secret, "HOW TO TRAIN YOUR HUMAN" book we bought off of the internet?!
Yee HAW!
"HOW 2 TRAIN your HUMAN BEAN"!
Ritten & illustrated by: Toots & Doo-Doo
sit-stay-ok... good human! here's a treat!
TOOTS! They're obeying me!
NO-Doo-Doo! Humans already sit when they eat!
clink!
(Treat)

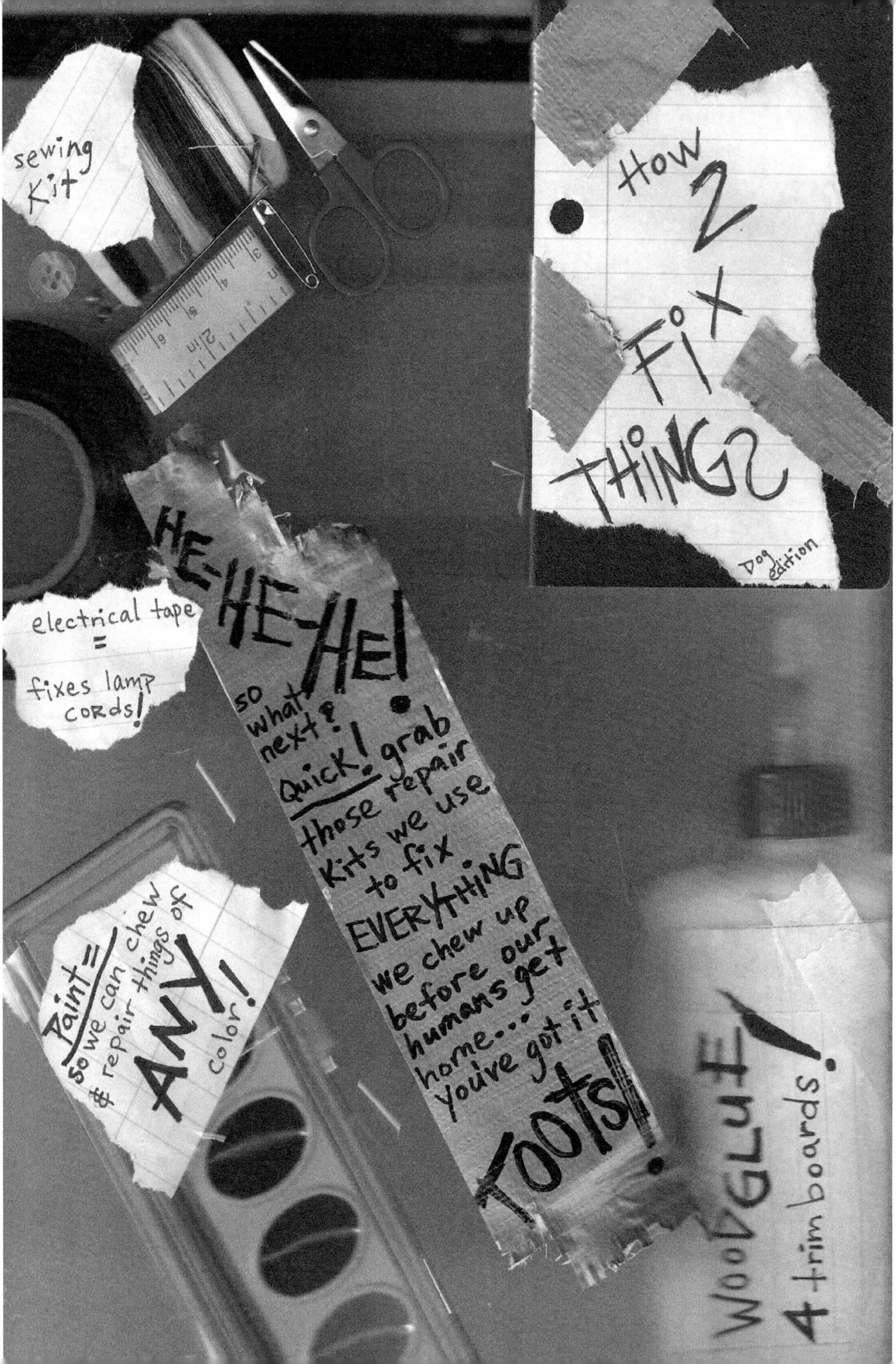
How 2 Fix Thingz
Dog edition
sewing Kit
electrical tape = fixes lamp cords!
HE-HE-HE!
so what next? Quick! grab those repair Kits we use to fix EVERYTHING we chew up before our humans get home... you've got it TOOTS!
Paint = so we can chew & repair things of ANY color!
WOOD GLUE 4 trim boards!

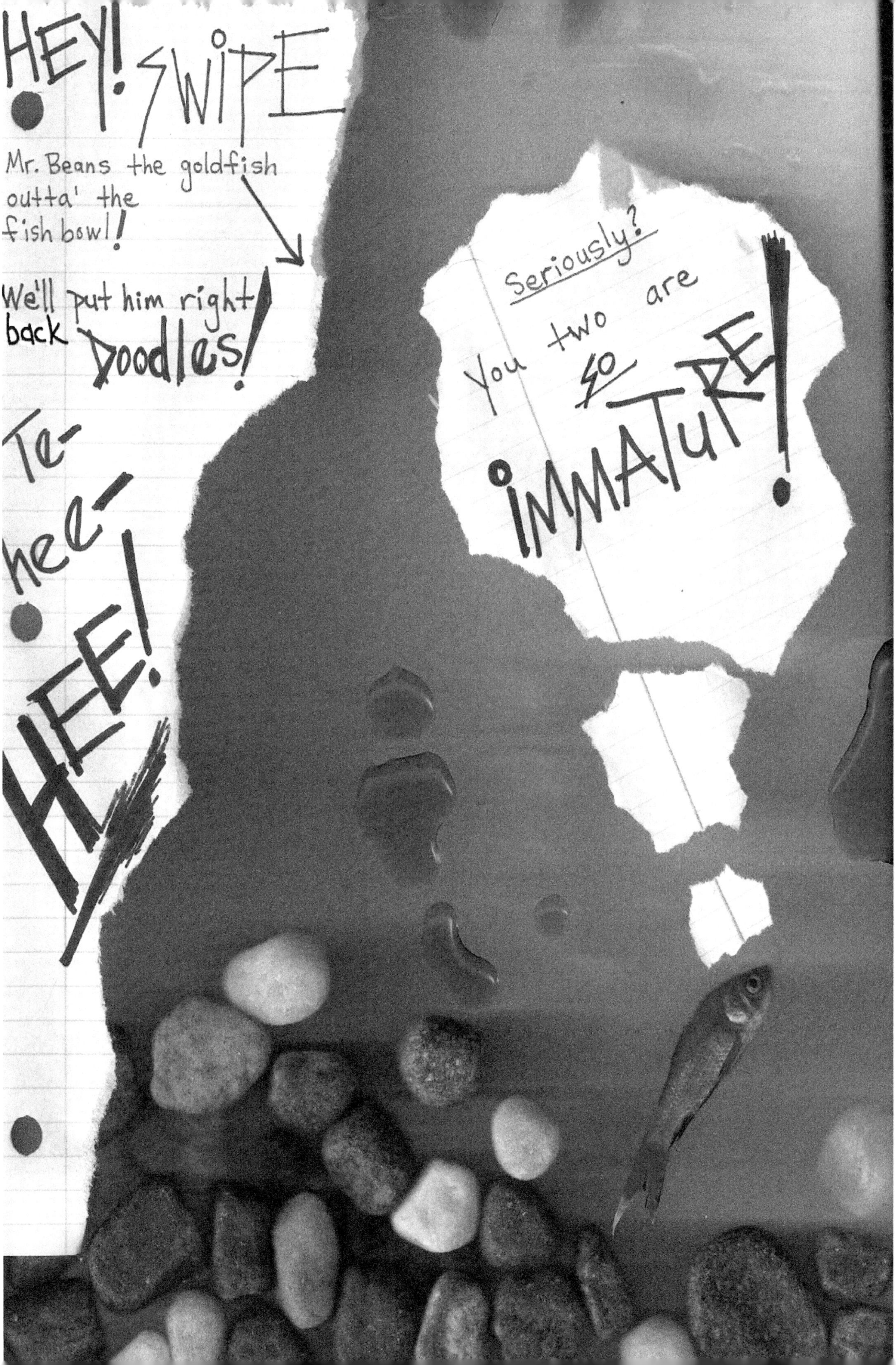
HEY! SWIPE
Mr. Beans the goldfish outta' the fish bowl!
We'll put him right back Doodles!
Te-hee-HEE!
Seriously? You two are so IMMATURE!

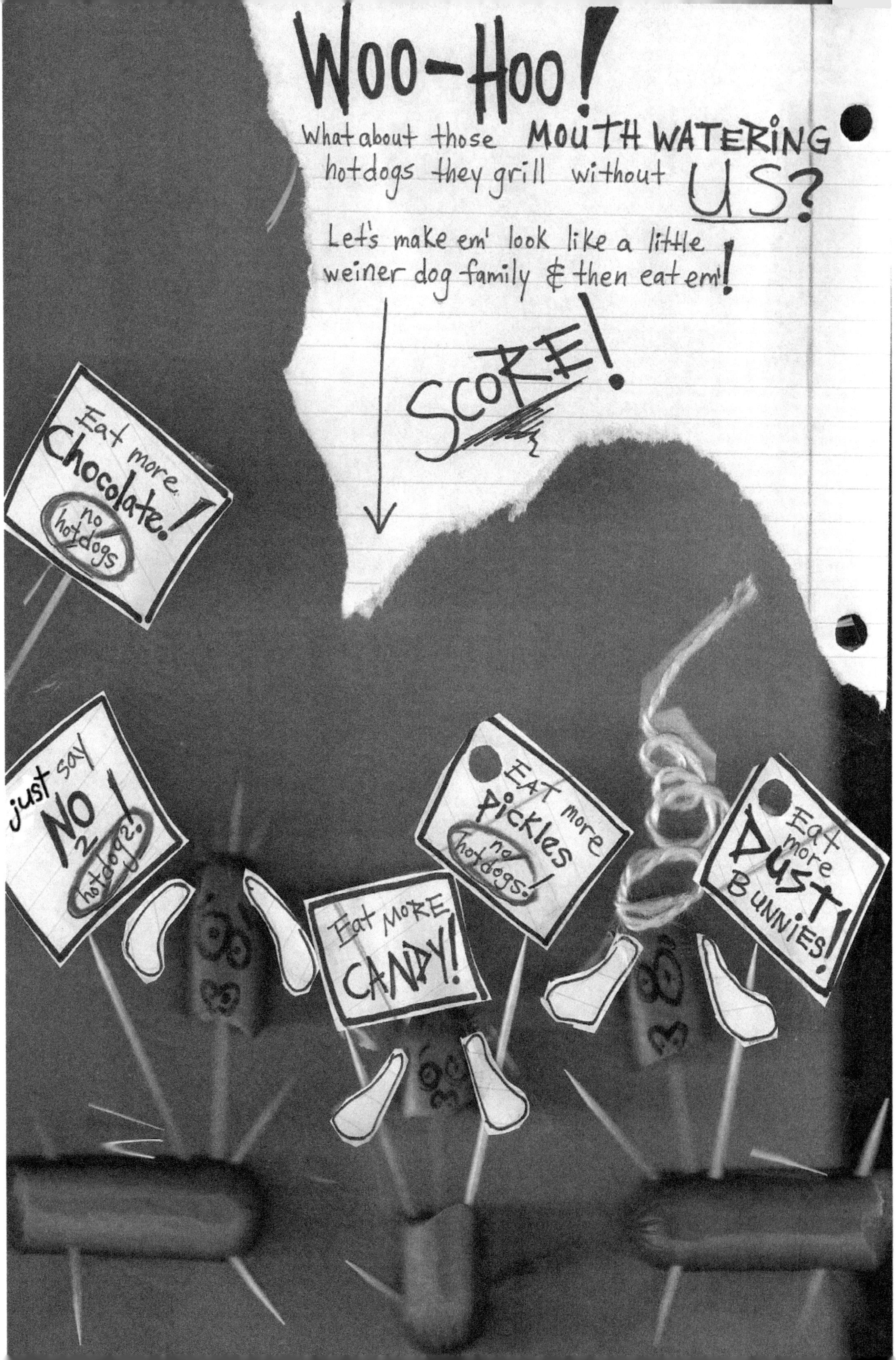

Woo-Hoo!
What about those MOUTH WATERING hotdogs they grill without US?
Let's make em' look like a little weiner dog family & then eat em'!
SCORE!
Eat more Chocolate! no hotdogs
just say NO 2 hotdogs?
Eat MORE CANDY!
EAT more Pickles no hotdogs!
Eat more DUST BUNNIES!

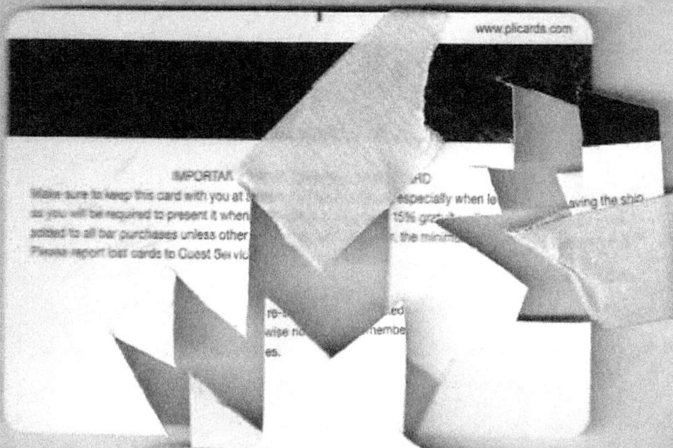
www.plicards.com

ooo! ooooooo!

DRAW A FUNNY picture of those credit cards we chewed up one Christmas so they'd spend more $money on US and less on family!... hehehe!

They'll never notice that we taped it! ↖

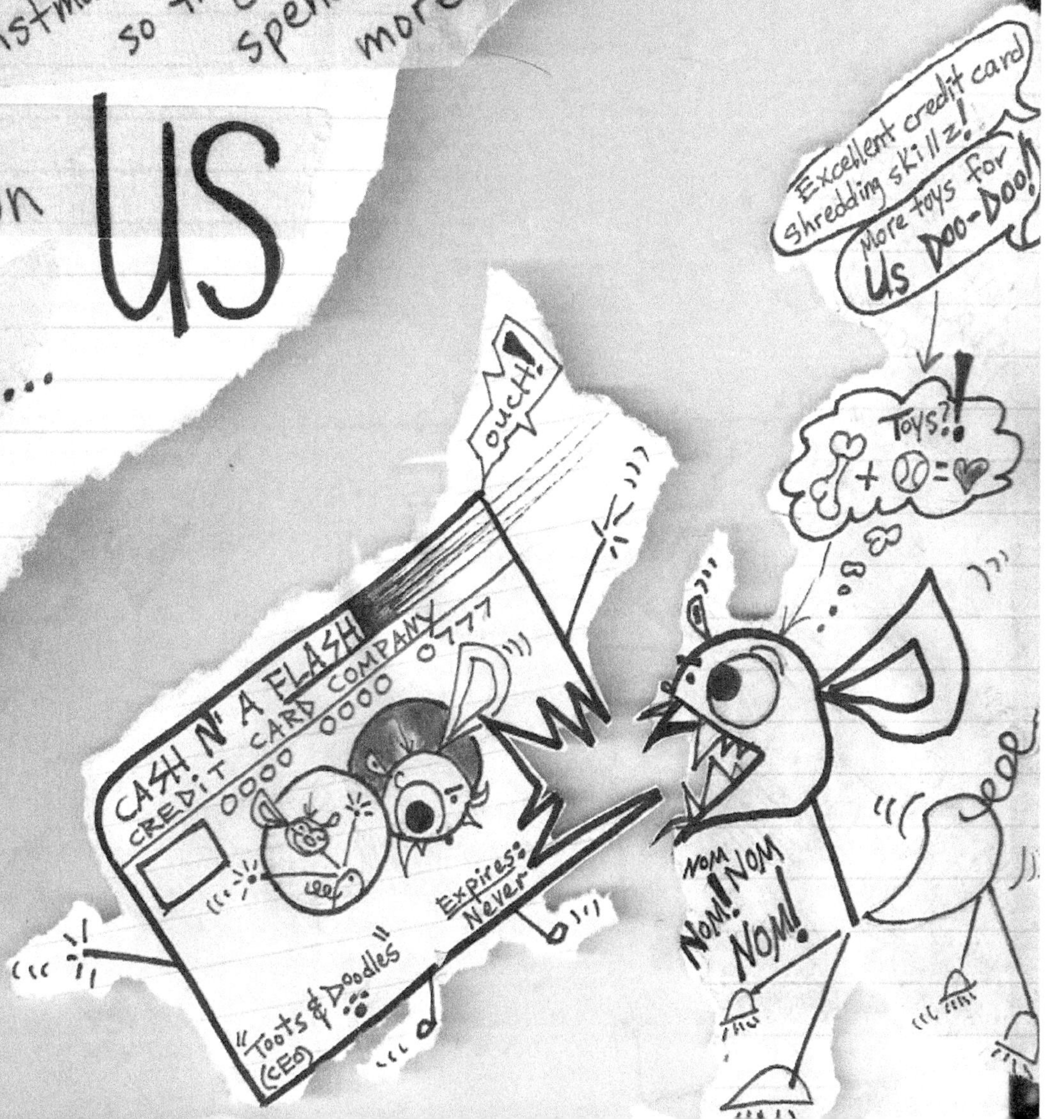
Excellent credit card shredding skillz!
More toys for US DOO-DOO!
Toys?!
ouch!
CASH N' A FLASH
CREDIT CARD COMPANY
0000 0000 0777
Expires: Never
"Toots & Doodles" (CEO)
NOM NOM NOM! NOM!

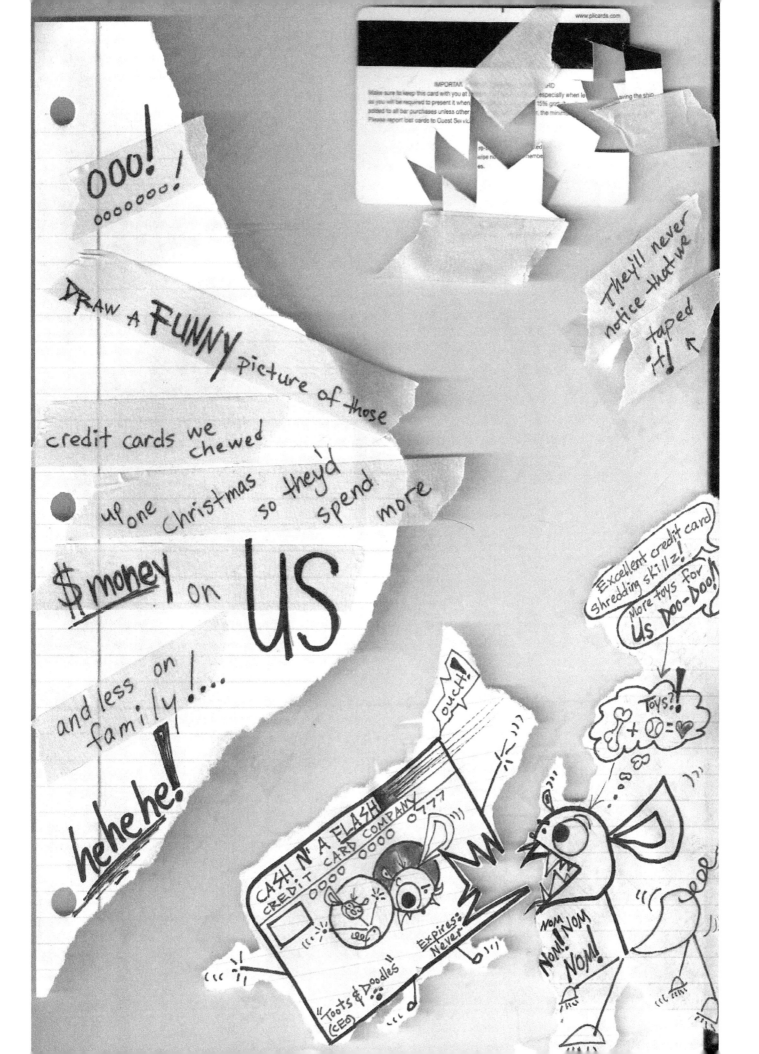

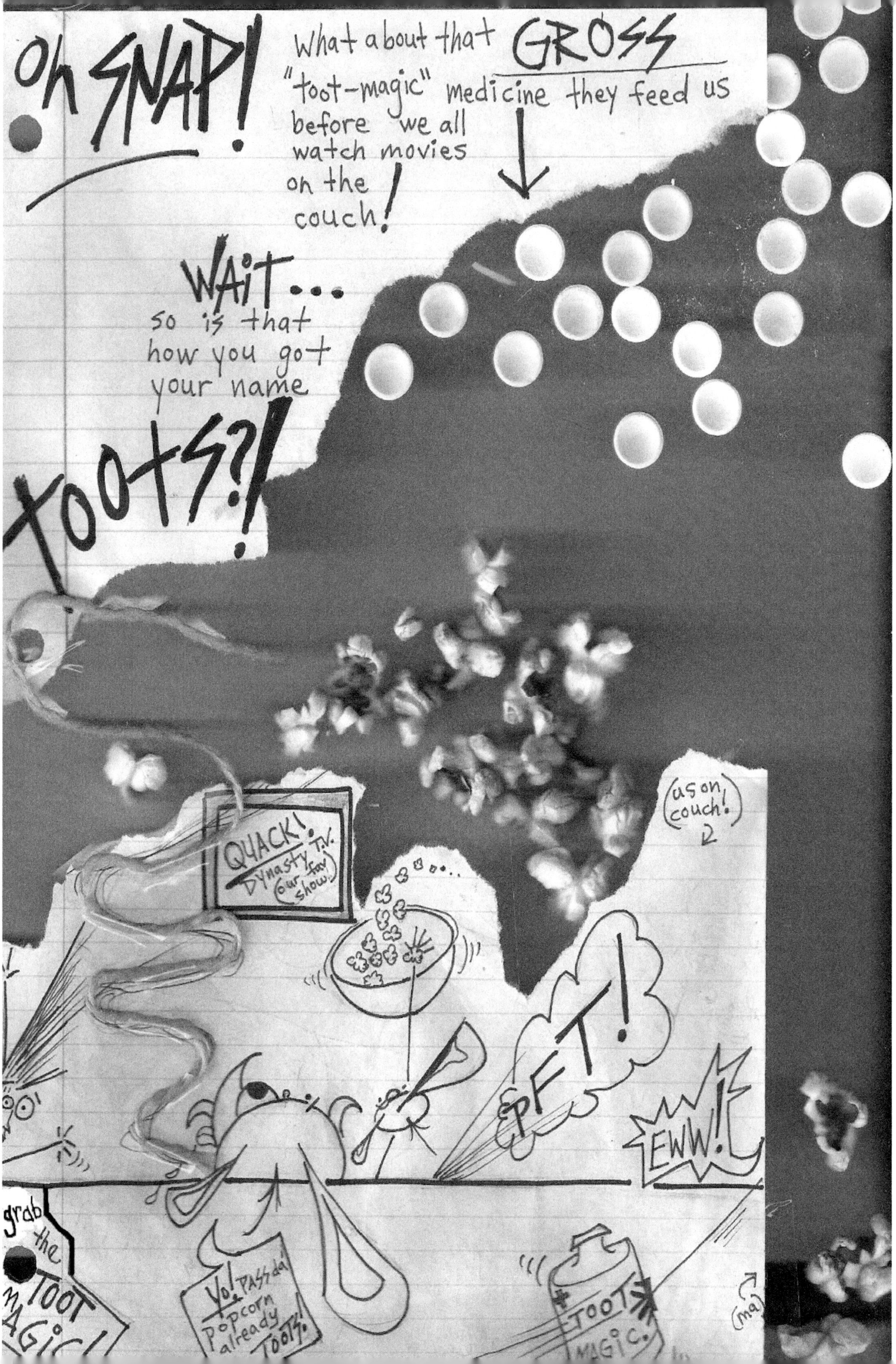

Oh SNAP!
What about that GROSS "toot-magic" medicine they feed us before we all watch movies on the couch!
WAIT... so is that how you got your name
TOOTS?!
(us on couch!)
QUACK! Dynasty T.V. (our fav show!)
PFT!
EWW!
grab the TOOT MAGIC!
Yo! PASS da popcorn already TOOTS!
TOOT MAGIC.

Dear. Jelly & Hairball,
We believe we speak 4 the whole houze— ride that dumb wheel again & we're bringing in the snakes from "run AWAY" Zoo!
signed—2 Tired pups
Toots & Doodles
AKA (Doo-Doo)

WiLL WERK 4 gerbils.

PS: We're leaving you a dumbell — start lifting weights or something!

Quick!

GRAB Jelly the gerbil and Hairball the hamster! No...they'd never stay, let's scan a funny picture and

TAPE it

to their cage so they won't keep us up **EVERY** night on that dumb wheel-of-torture!

TeE-He-HEE!

da-da-dun! da-da-dun! da-da-DUN-DUN-DUN! gotta-run! gotta-run! gotta-RUN-RUN-RUN!
(even smaller brain)
(Mr. Beans old cracked fish tank.)
Hi.
Hairball
ooo! ooo! ME NEXT! ME NEXT!
H_2O
(small brain)
JELLY

Hamster bedding?! I'm SO not jealous!

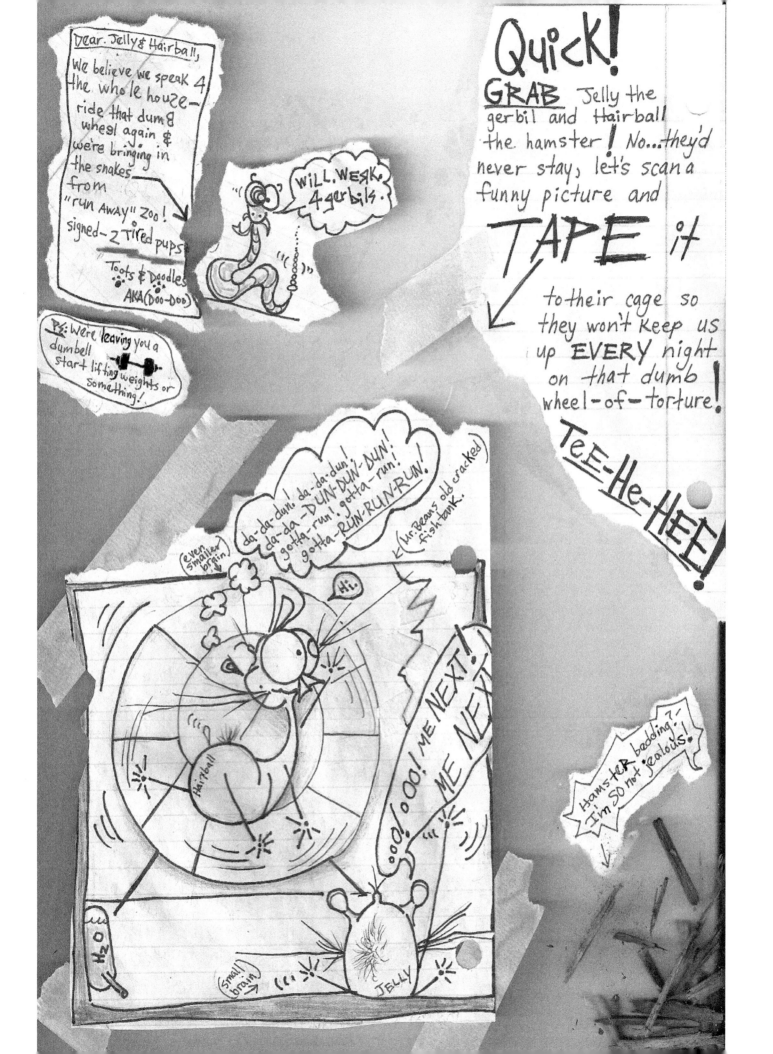

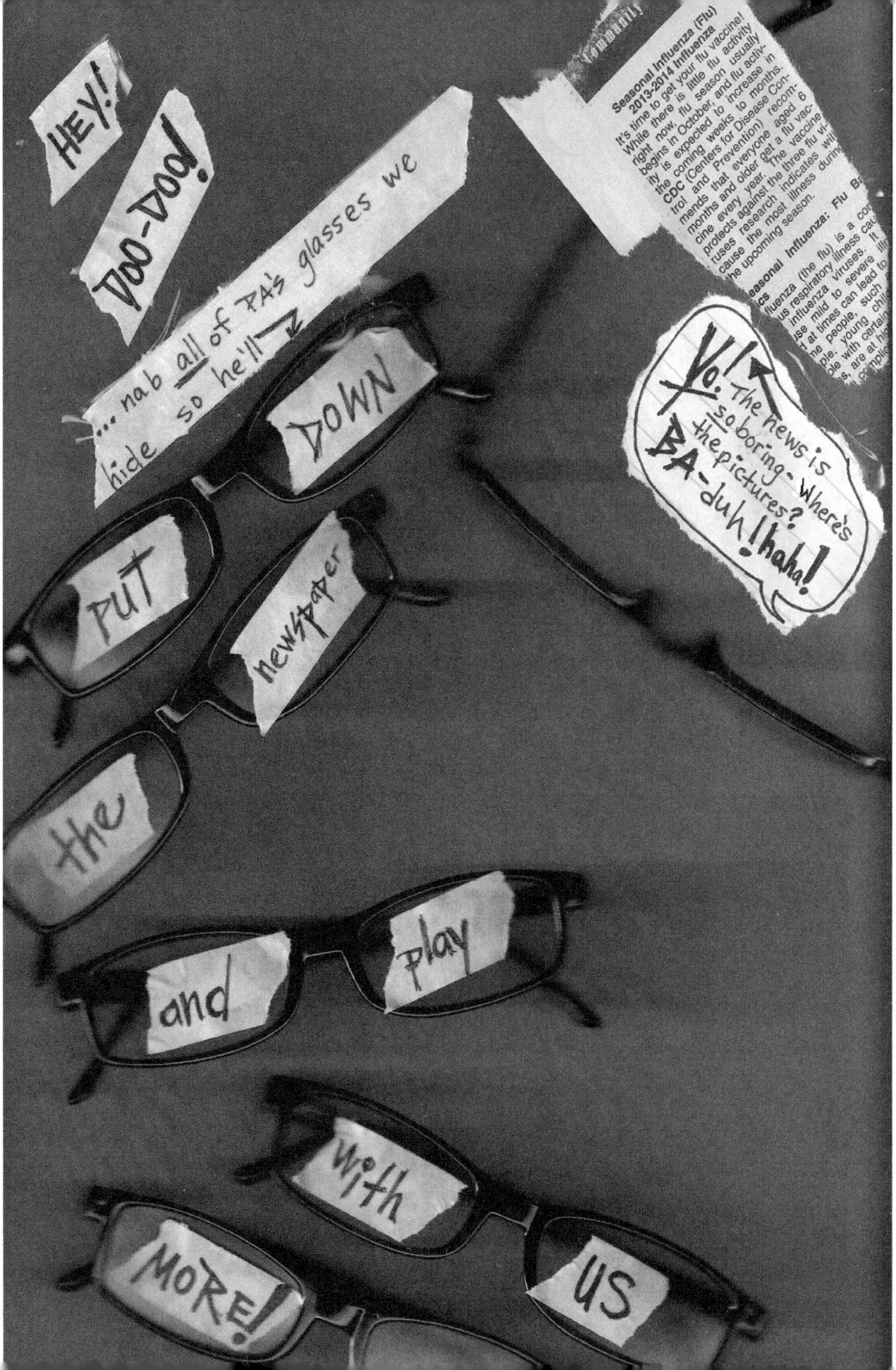
HEY!
DOO-DOO!
...nab all of PA's glasses we hide so he'll
PUT DOWN the newspaper and play with us MORE!
Seasonal Influenza (Flu) 2013-2014 Influenza
It's time to get your flu vaccine! While there is little flu activity right now, flu season usually begins in October, and flu activity is expected to increase in the coming weeks to months. CDC (Centers for Disease Control and Prevention) recommends that everyone aged 6 months and older get a flu vaccine every year. The vaccine protects against the three flu viruses research indicates will cause the most illness during the upcoming season.
Yo! The news is so boring - where's the pictures? BA-duh! haha!

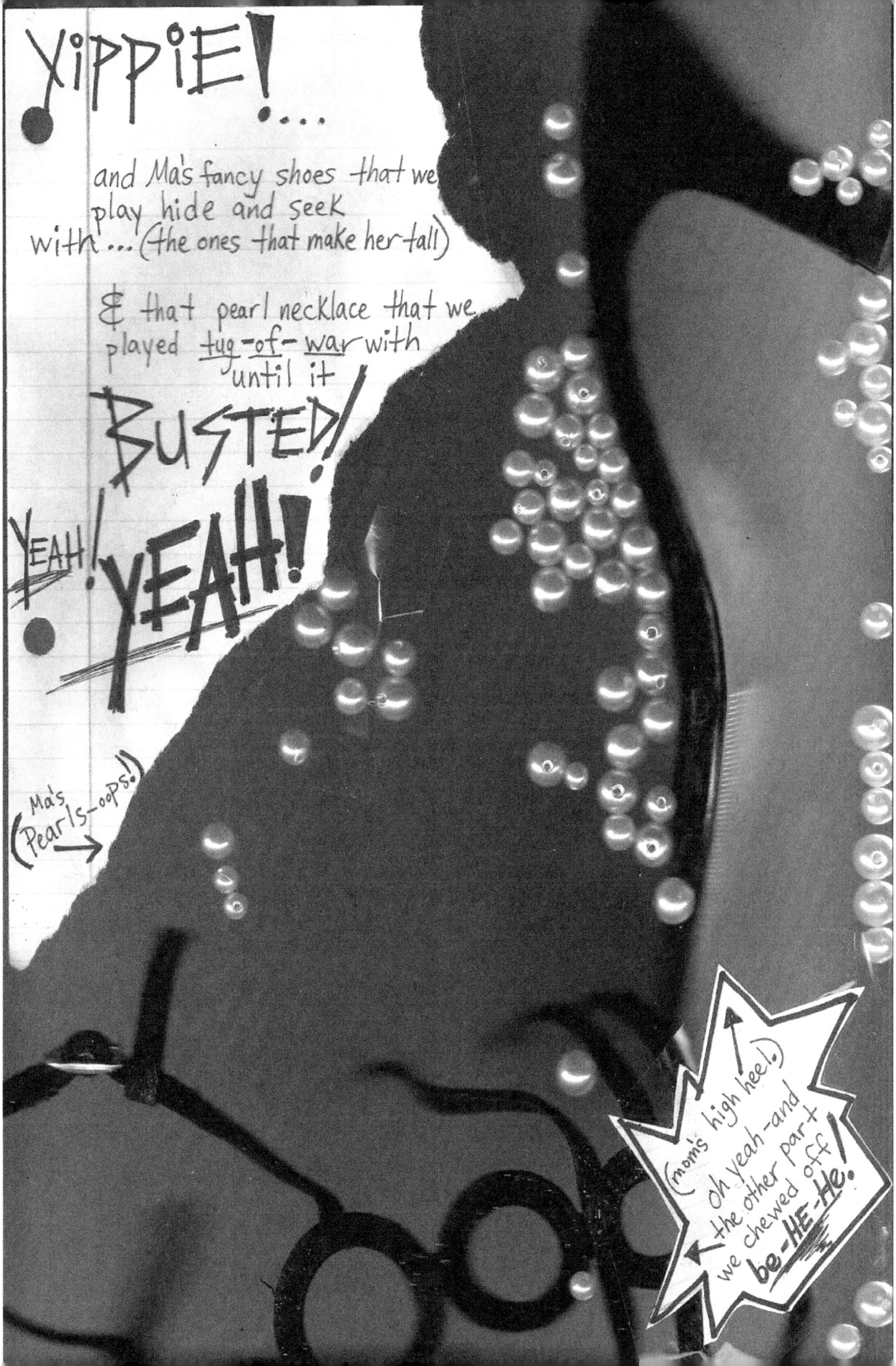
YiPPiE!...
and Ma's fancy shoes that we play hide and seek with... (the ones that make her tall)
& that pearl necklace that we played tug-of-war with until it
BUSTED!
YEAH! YEAH!
(Ma's Pearls-oops!)
(mom's high heel.) oh yeah-and the other part we chewed off! be-HE-He.

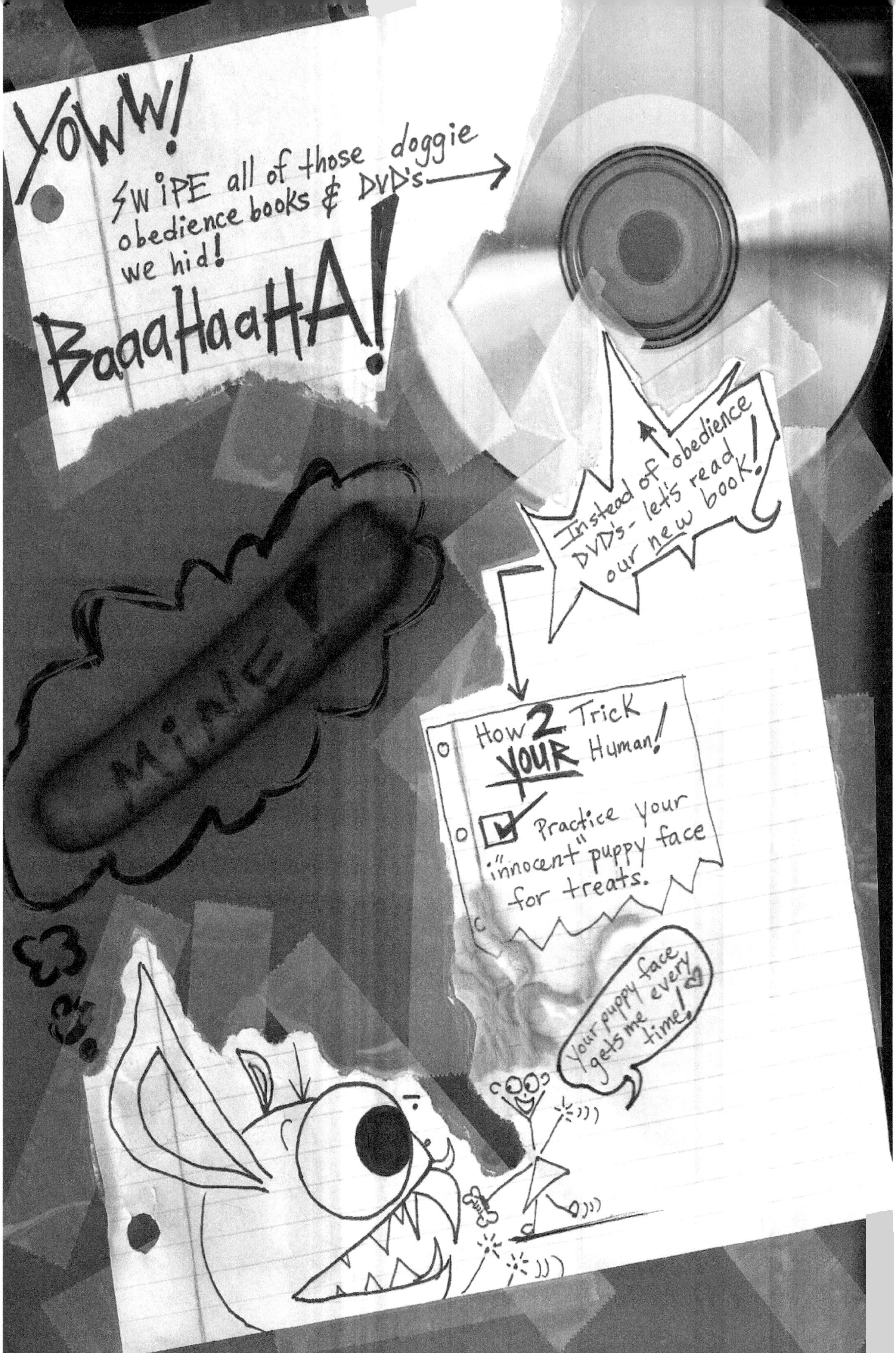
YOWW!
SWIPE all of those doggie obedience books & DVD's we hid!
BaaaHaaHA!
MINE!
Instead of obedience DVD's- let's read our new book!
How 2 Trick YOUR Human!
Practice your "innocent" puppy face for treats.
Your puppy face gets me every time!

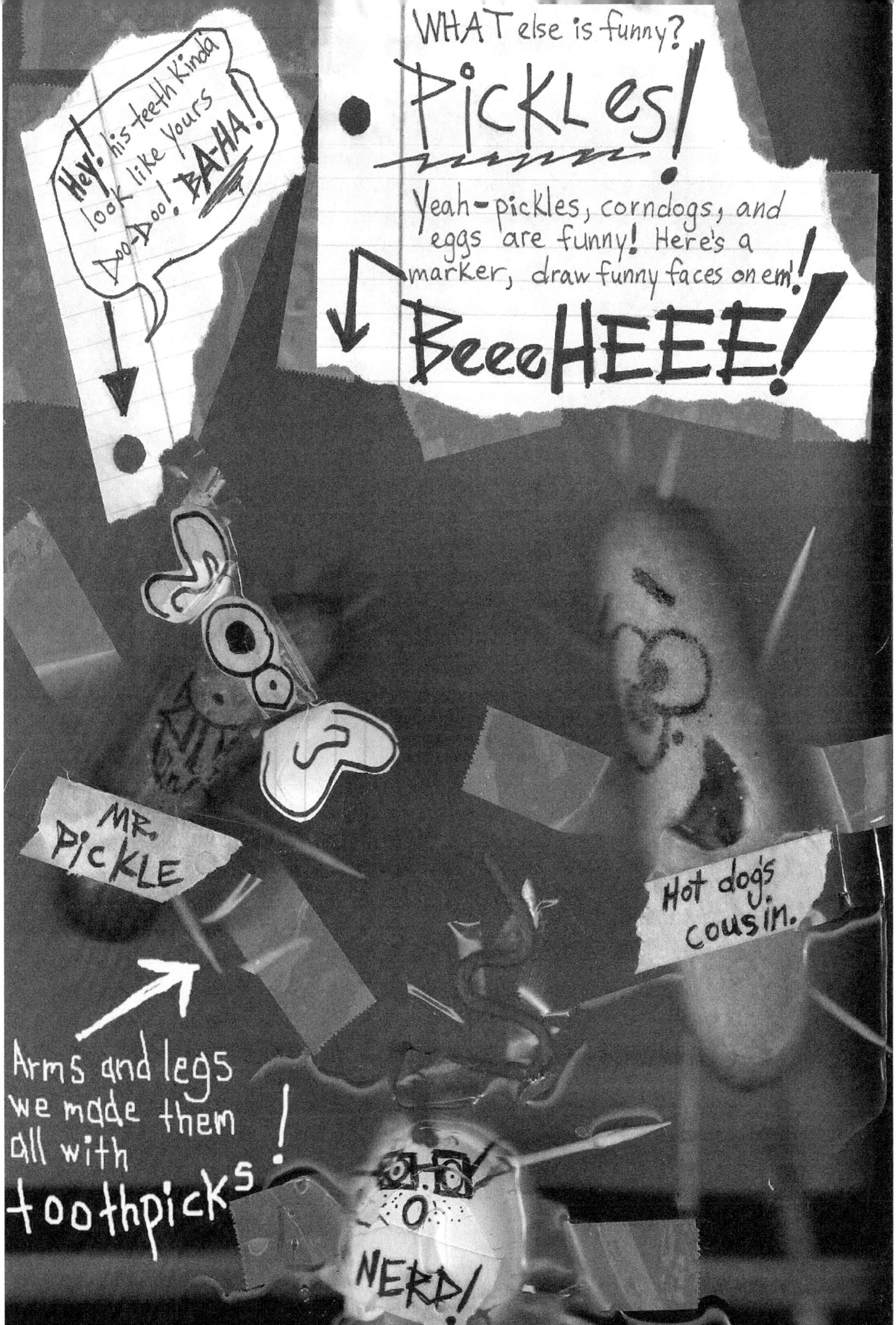
WHAT else is funny?
Pickles!
Yeah-pickles, corndogs, and eggs are funny! Here's a marker, draw funny faces on em'!
BeeeHEEE!
Hey! his teeth kinda look like yours Doo-Doo! BA-HA!
MR. PICKLE
Hot dog's cousin.
Arms and legs we made them all with toothpicks!
NERD!

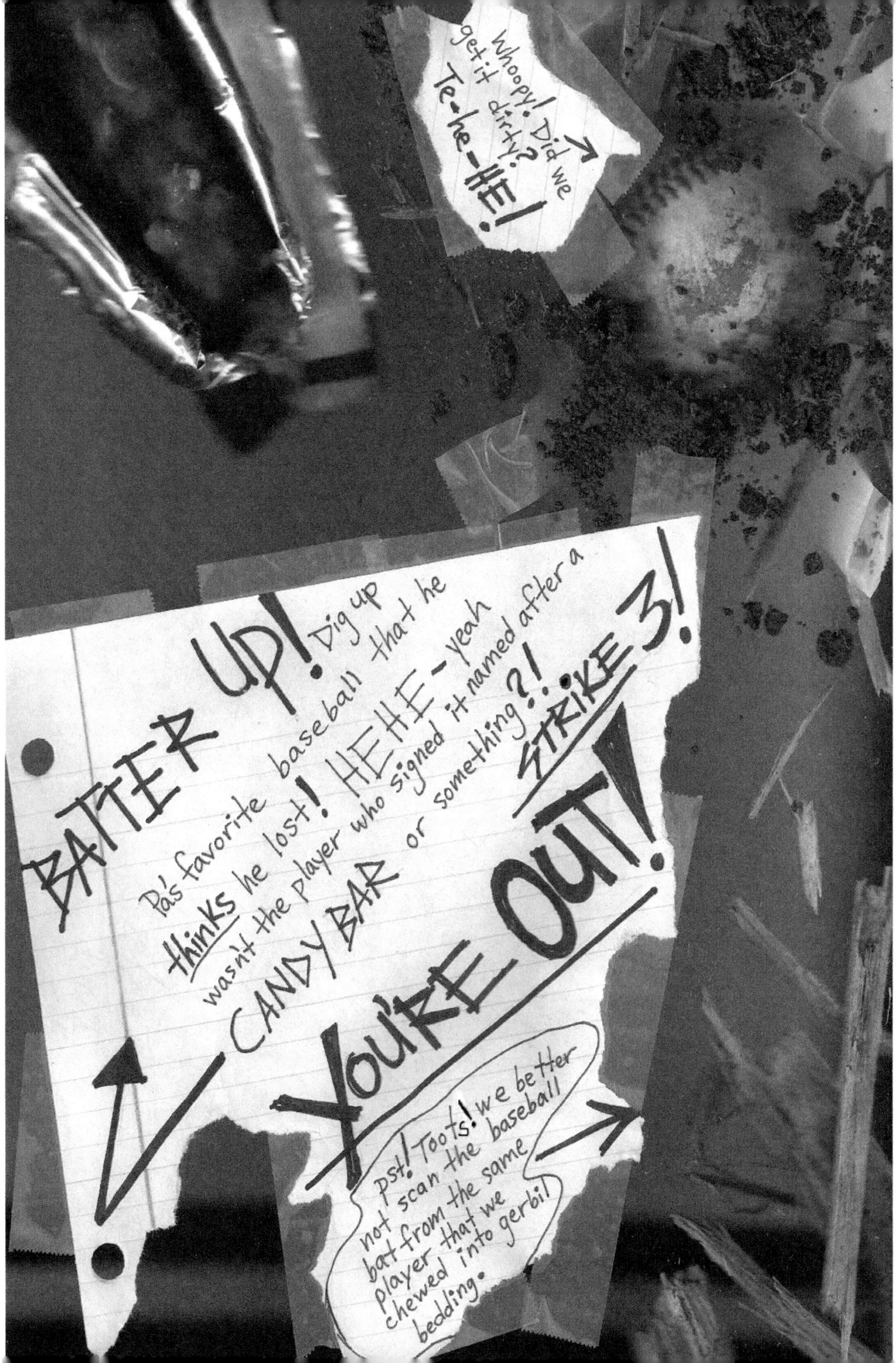
Whoopy! Did we get it dirty? Te-he-HE!
BATTER UP! Dig up Pa's favorite baseball that he thinks he lost! HEHE-yeah wasn't the player who signed it named after a CANDY BAR or something?!..
STRIKE 3!
YOU'RE OUT!
pst! Toots! we better not scan the baseball bat from the same player that we chewed into gerbil bedding.

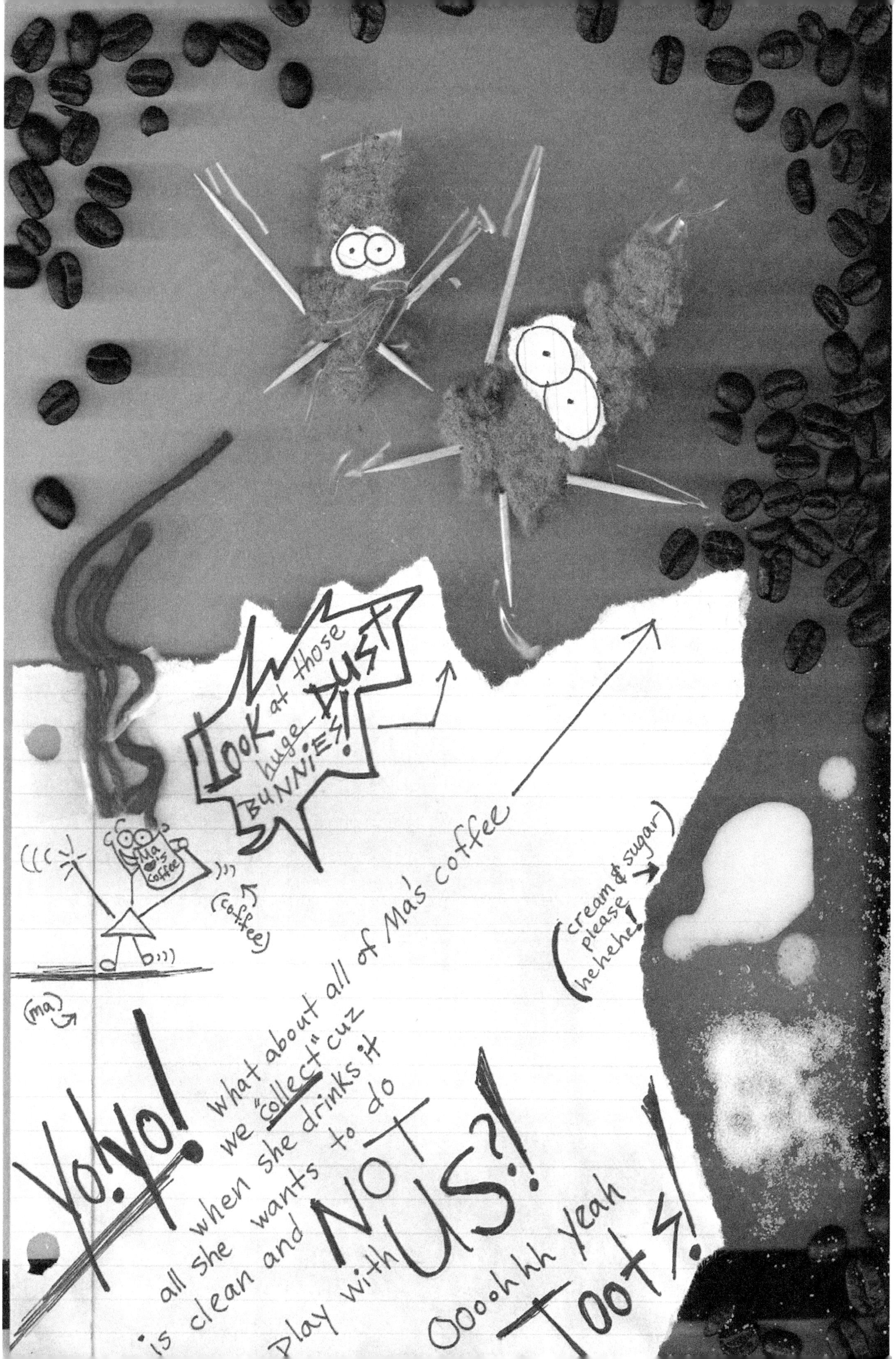

Look at those huge DUST BUNNIES!
Ma's coffee
(coffee)
(ma)
Yo! Yo!
what about all of Ma's coffee
we "collect" cuz
when she drinks it
all she wants to do
is clean and NOT
play with US?!
(cream & sugar please hehehe!)
Ooooh hh yeah Toots!

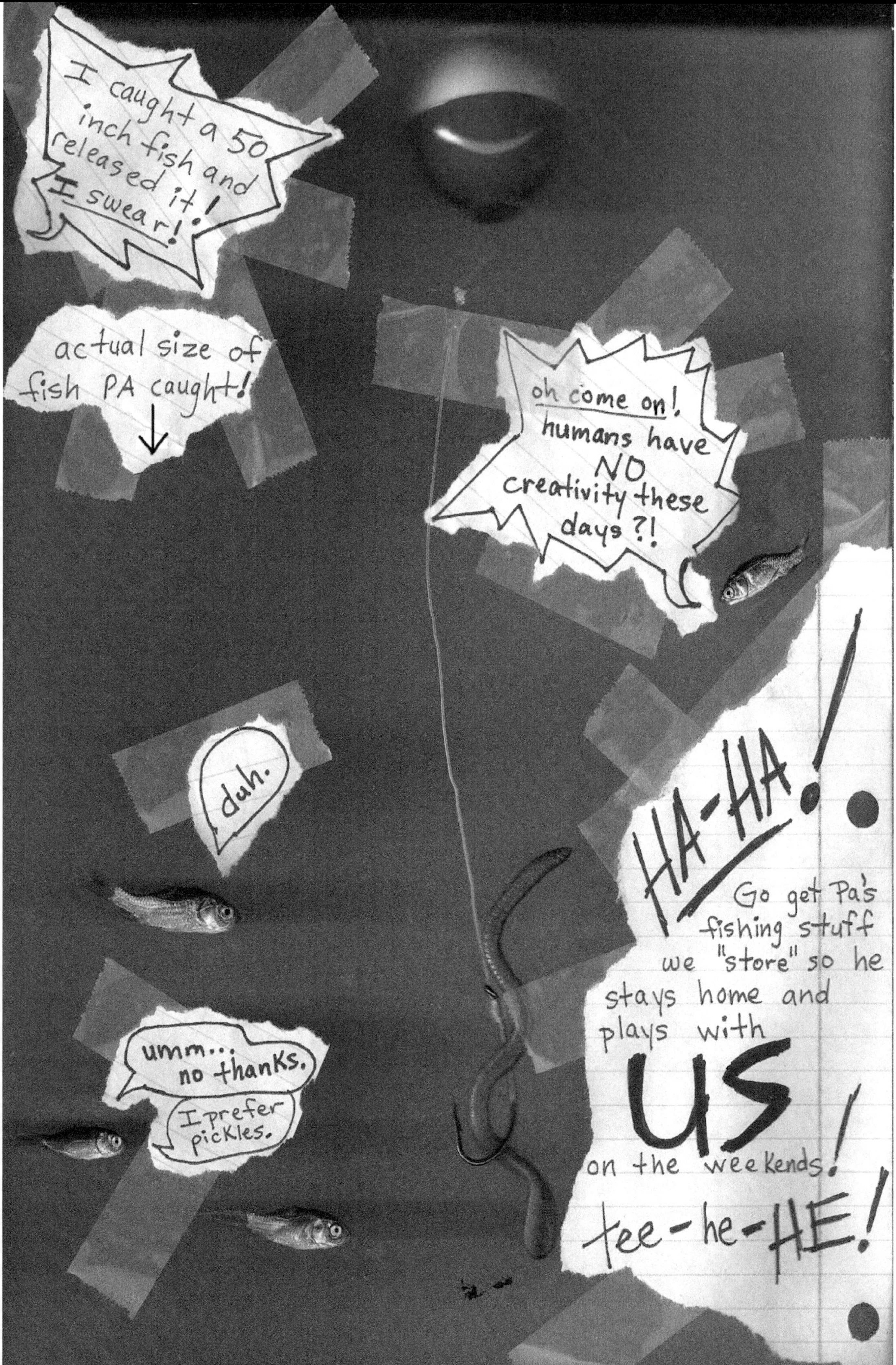
I caught a 50 inch fish and released it! I swear!
actual size of fish PA caught!
oh come on! humans have NO creativity these days?!
duh.
umm... no thanks.
I prefer pickles.
HA-HA!
Go get Pa's fishing stuff we "store" so he stays home and plays with US! on the weekends!
tee-he-HE!

YO! DOO-DOO!

What about all the shampoo bottles we emptied so we don't have to take as many baths?!

← icky (soap!)

"R" problem!

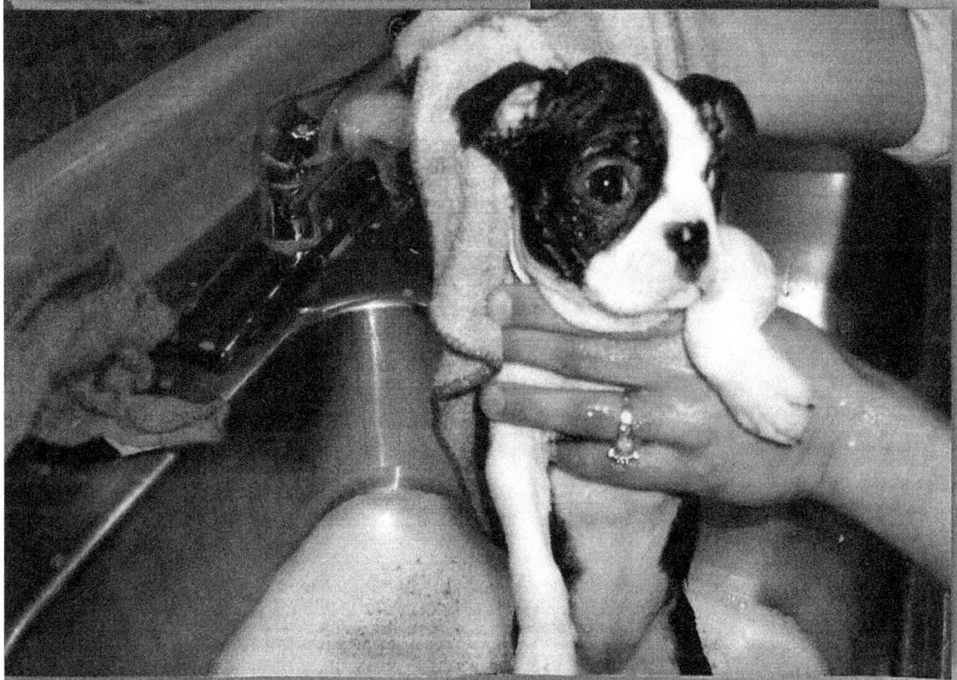

"R" solution!

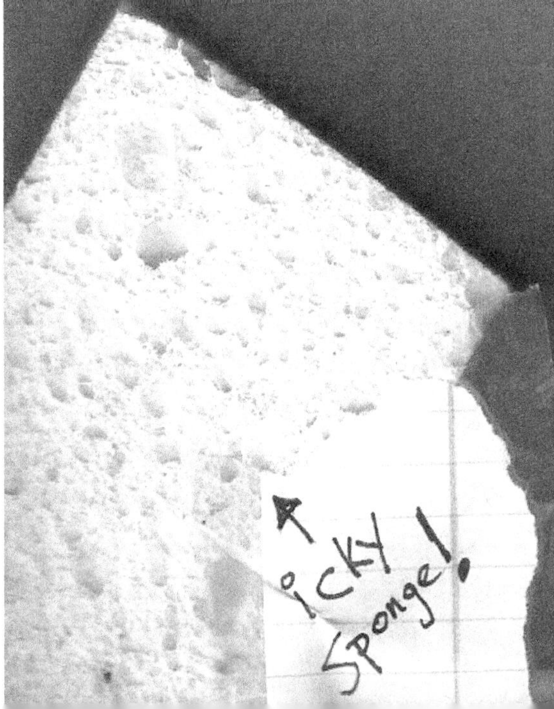

↑ icky sponge!

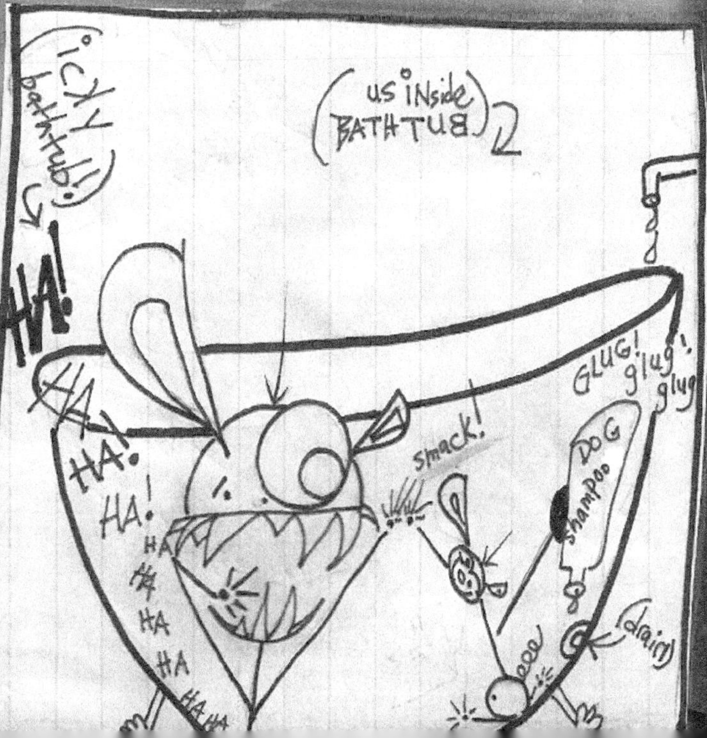

(icky bathtub!)
(us inside BATHTUB)
HA!
HA
HA!
HA!
HA
HA
HA
HA
smack!
GLUG! glug! glug
DOG shampoo
(drain)

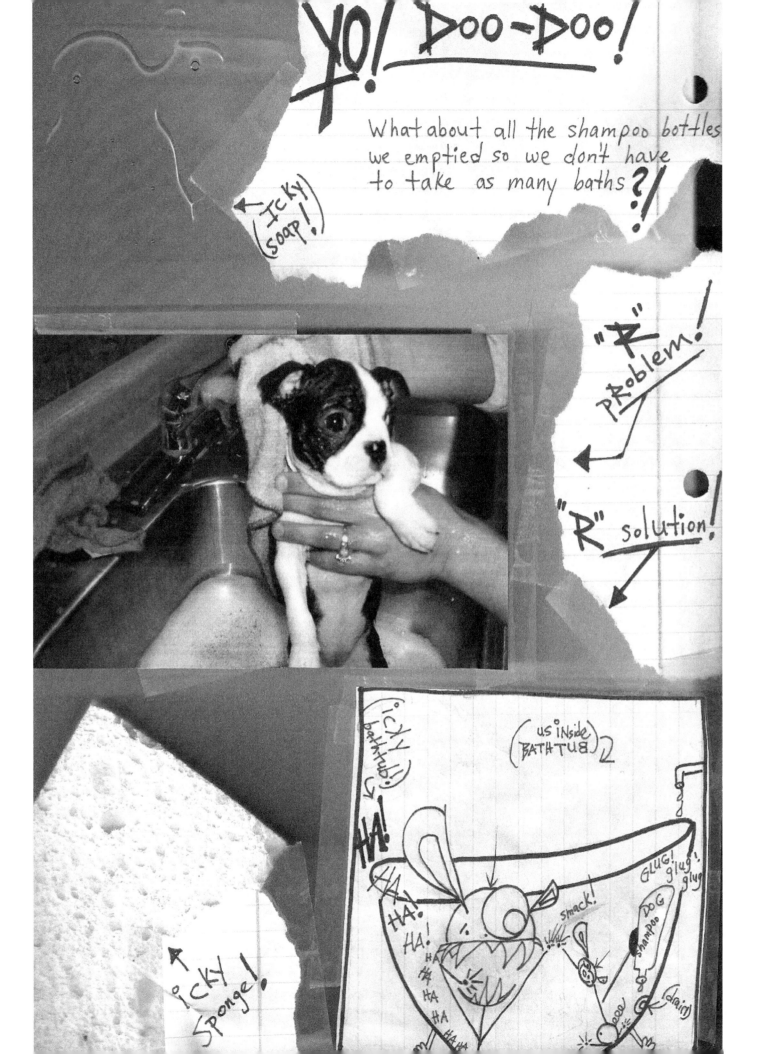

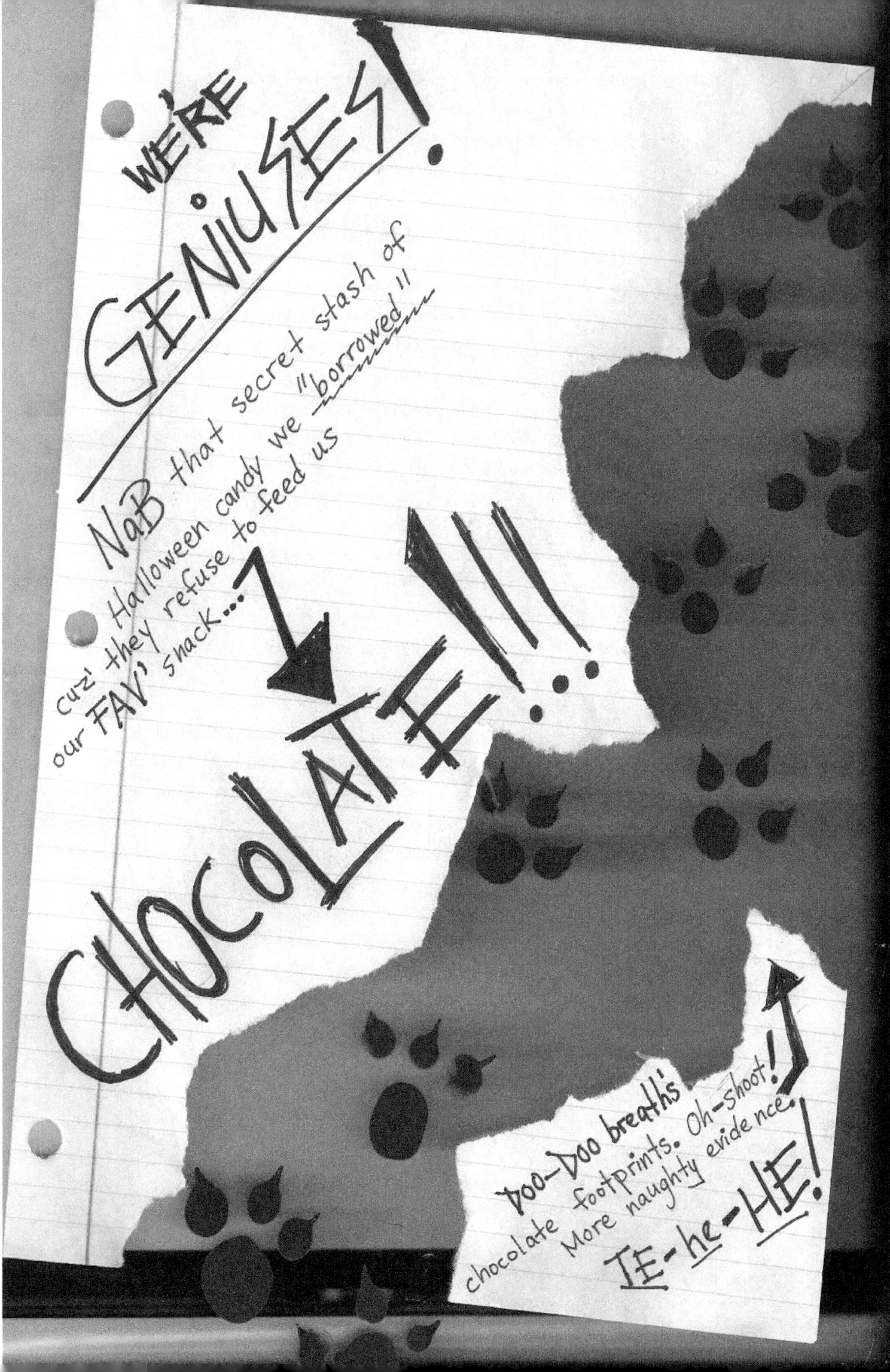
WE'RE GENIUSES!
NaB that secret stash of
Halloween candy we "borrowed"
cuz' they refuse to feed us
our FAV' snack...
CHOCOLATE!!!
Doo-Doo breath's
chocolate footprints. Oh-shoot!
More naughty evidence.
IE-he-HE!

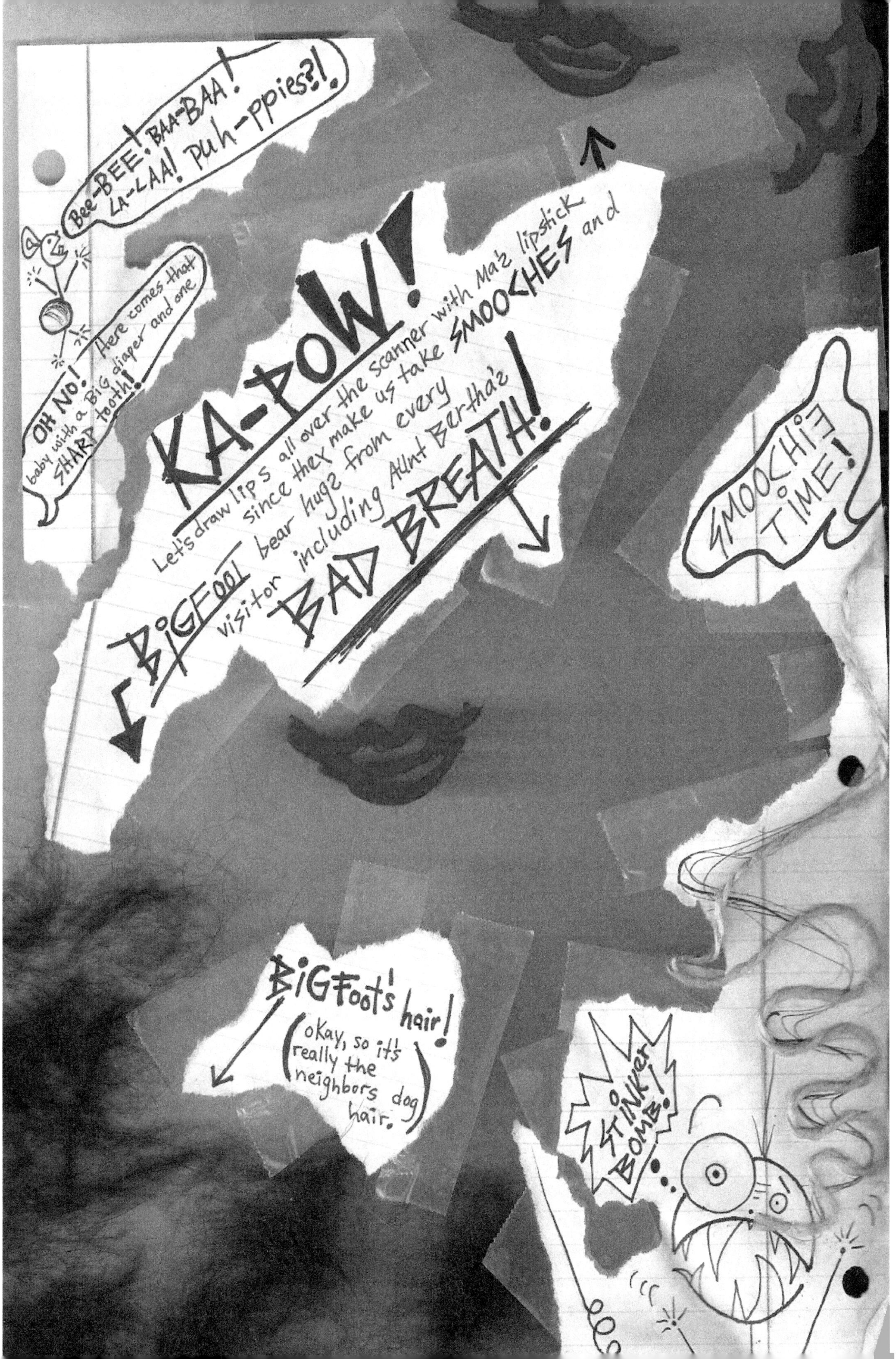

Bee-BEE! BAA-BAA! LA-LAA! puh-ppies?!.
OH NO! Here comes that baby with a BIG diaper and one SHARP tooth!
KA-POW!
Let's draw lips all over the scanner with Ma's lipstick since they make us take SMOOCHES and bear hugs from every visitor including Aunt Bertha's BAD BREATH!
BIGFOOT
SMOOCHIE TIME!
BIGFoot's hair! (okay, so it's really the neighbors dog hair.)
STINKer BOMB!

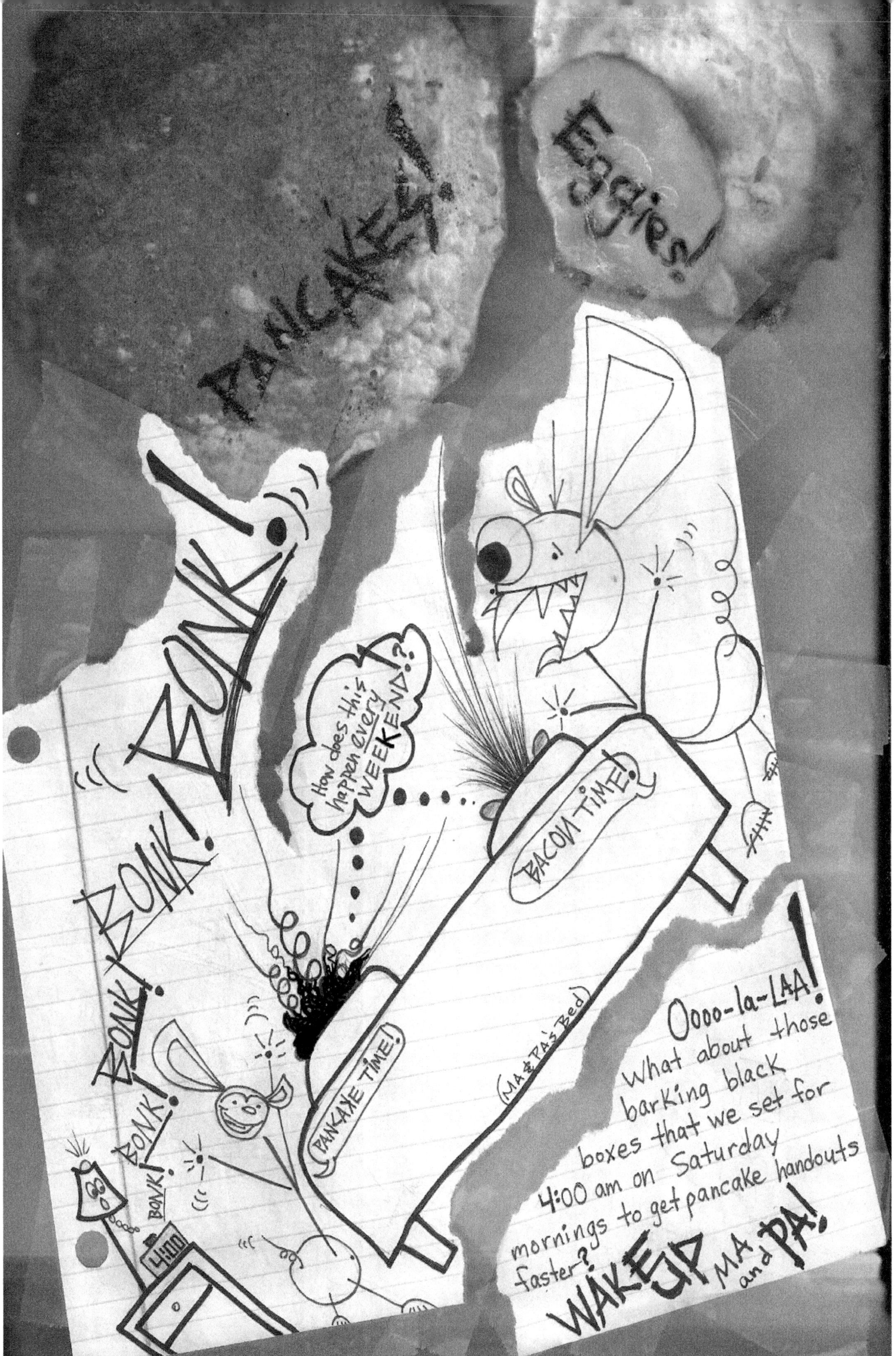
PANCAKES!
Eggies!
BONK! BONK! BONK!
BONK! BONK!
BONK!
How does this happen every WEEKEND?!
BACON TIME!
PANCAKE TIME!
(MA & PA's Bed)
4:00
Oooo-la-LAA!
What about those barking black boxes that we set for 4:00 am on Saturday mornings to get pancake handouts faster?
WAKE UP MA and PA!

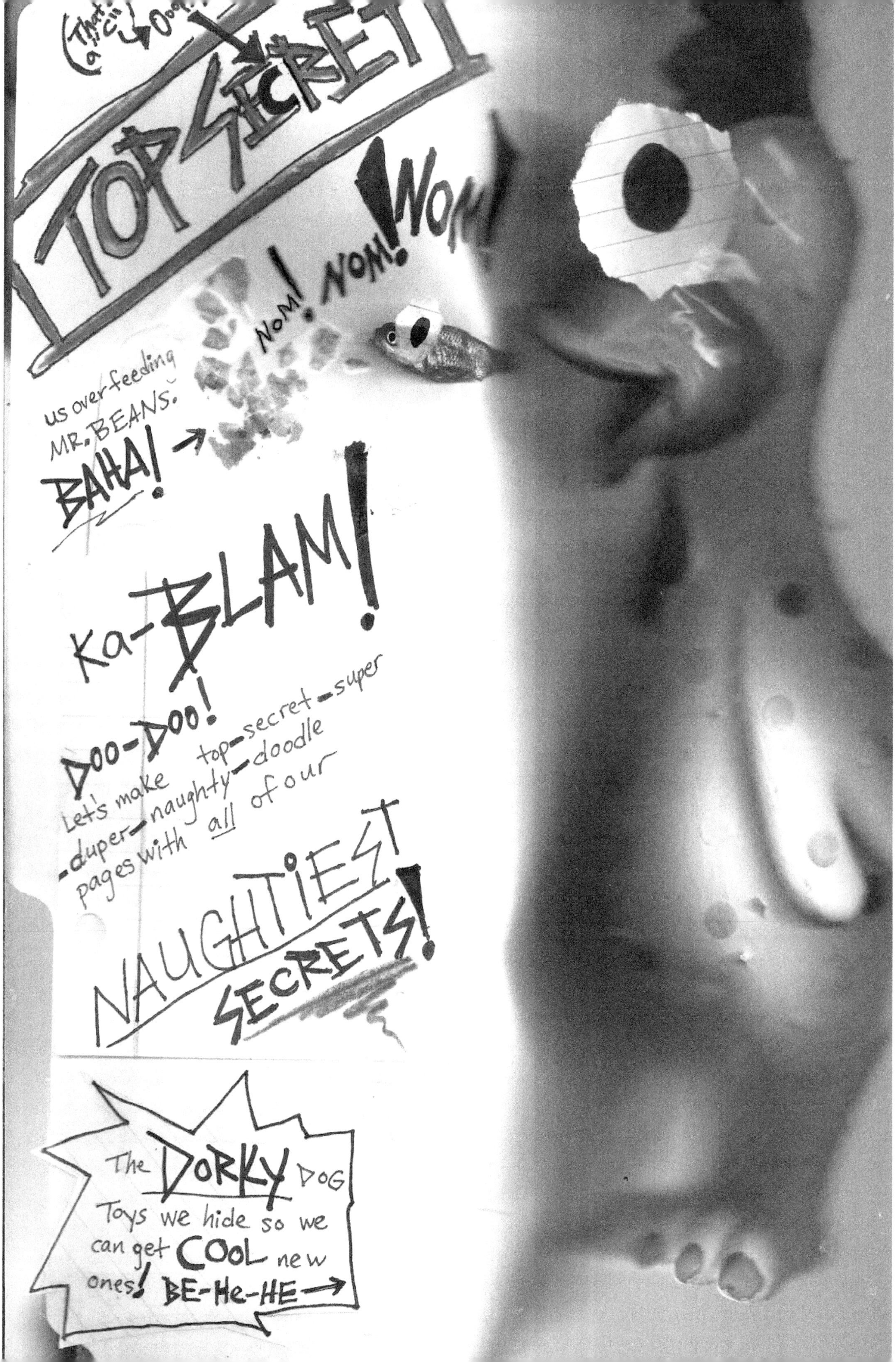

(That's a "C" Ooo...
TOP SECRET
NOM! NOM! NOM!
us over-feeding MR. BEANS.
BAHA!
Ka-BLAM!
DOO-DOO!
Let's make top-secret-super-duper-naughty-doodle pages with all of our
NAUGHTIEST SECRETS!
The DORKY DOG
Toys we hide so we can get COOL new ones! BE-He-HE

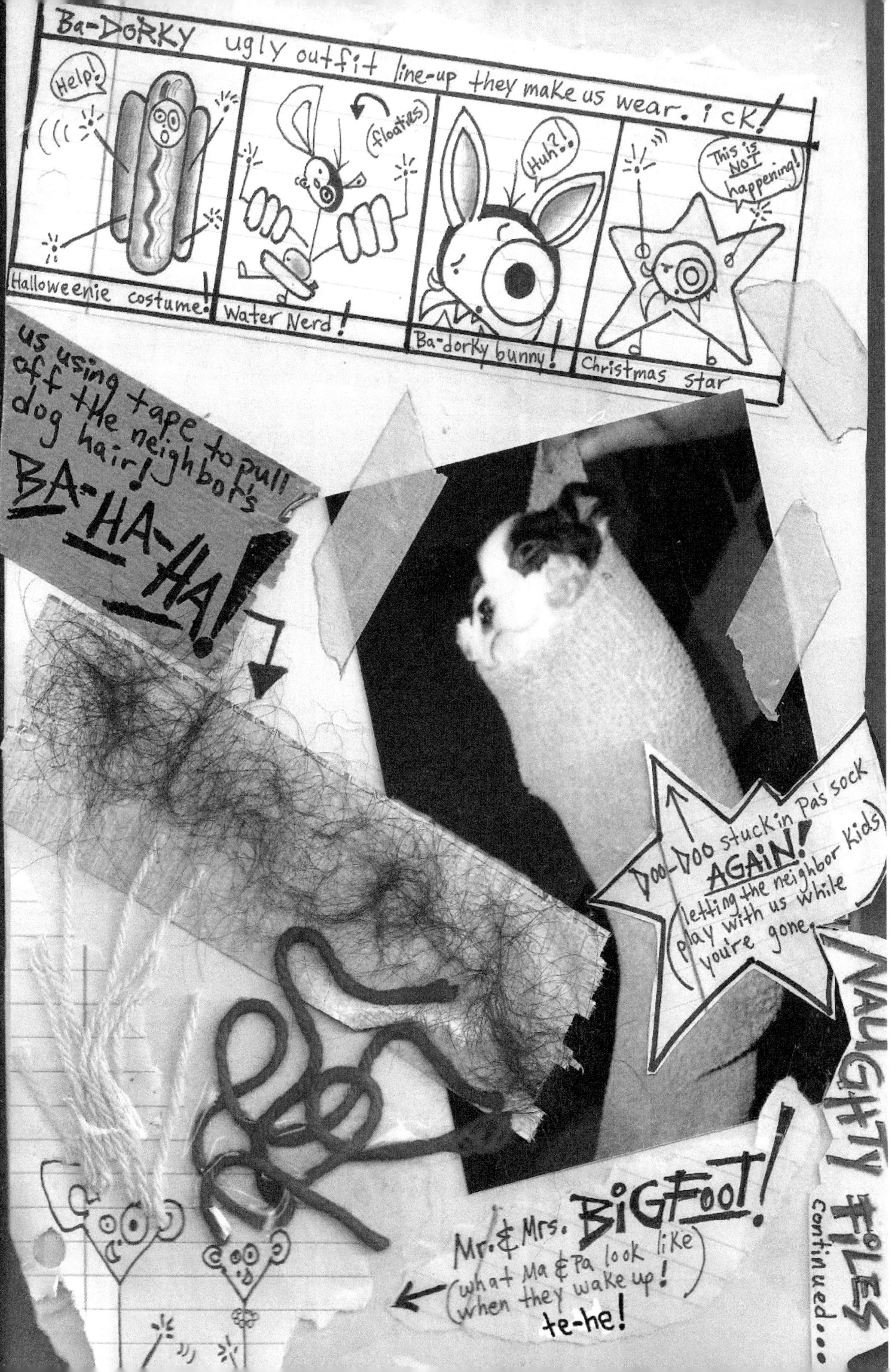
Ba-DORKY ugly outfit line-up they make us wear. ick!
Help!
Halloweenie costume!
floaties
Water Nerd!
Huh?!
Ba-dorky bunny!
This is NOT happening!
Christmas star
us using tape to pull off the neighbor's dog hair!
BA-HA-HA!
Doo-Doo stuck in Pa's sock AGAIN!
(letting the neighbor kids play with us while you're gone.)
NAUGHTY FILES
continued...
Mr. & Mrs. BiGFoot!
(what Ma & Pa look like when they wake up!)
te-he!

meanwhile... as ma & pa are enjoying a quiet dinner at a resturant...

ma gets a **MESSAGE!**

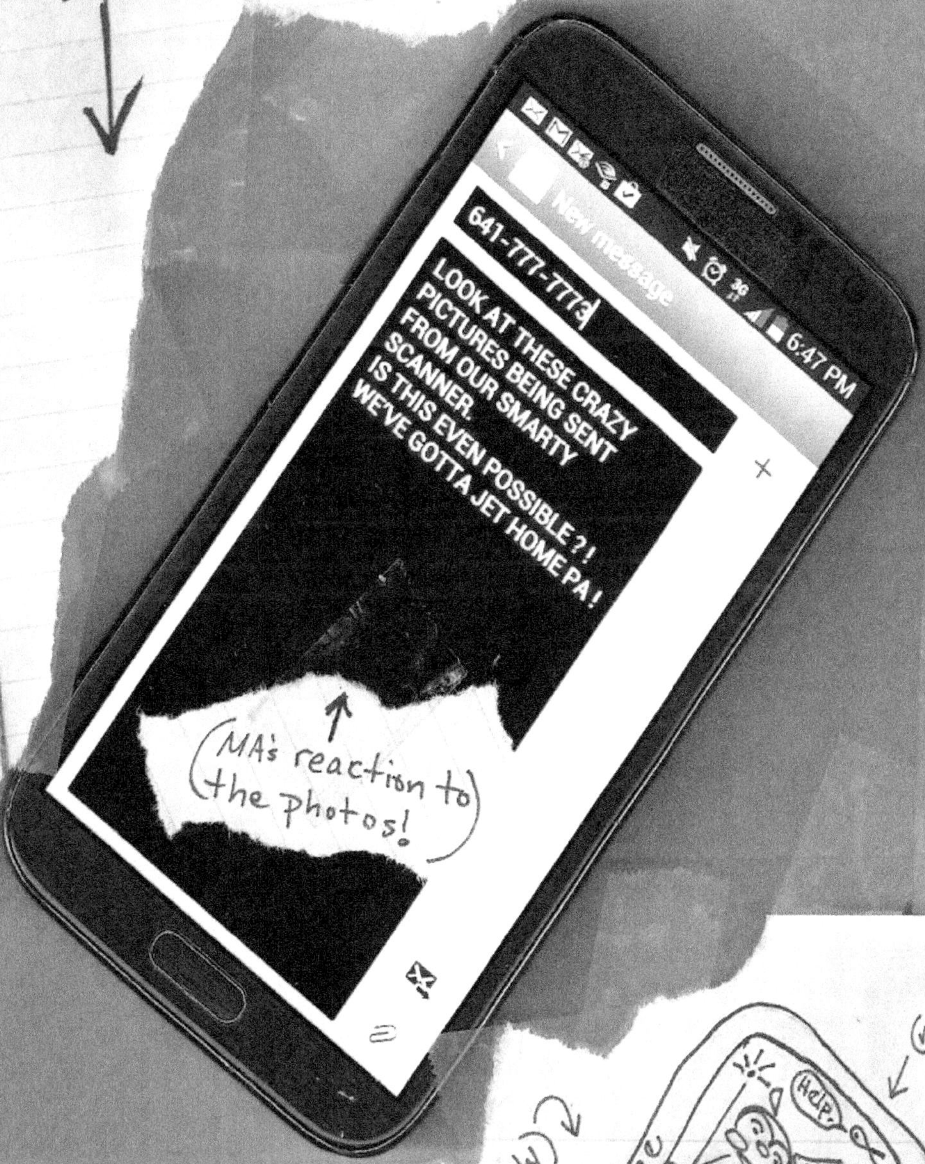
New message
6:47 PM
641-777-7773
LOOK AT THESE CRAZY PICTURES BEING SENT FROM OUR SMARTY SCANNER.
IS THIS EVEN POSSIBLE?!
WE'VE GOTTA JET HOME PA!
(MA's reaction to the photos!)

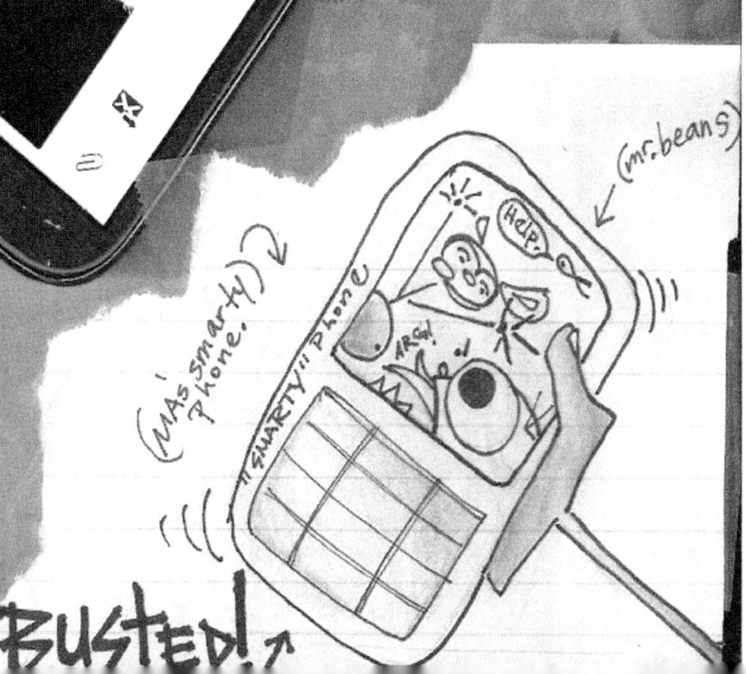
(mr. beans)
Help.
ARG!
(MA's smarty phone.)
"SMARTY" Phone
BUSTED!

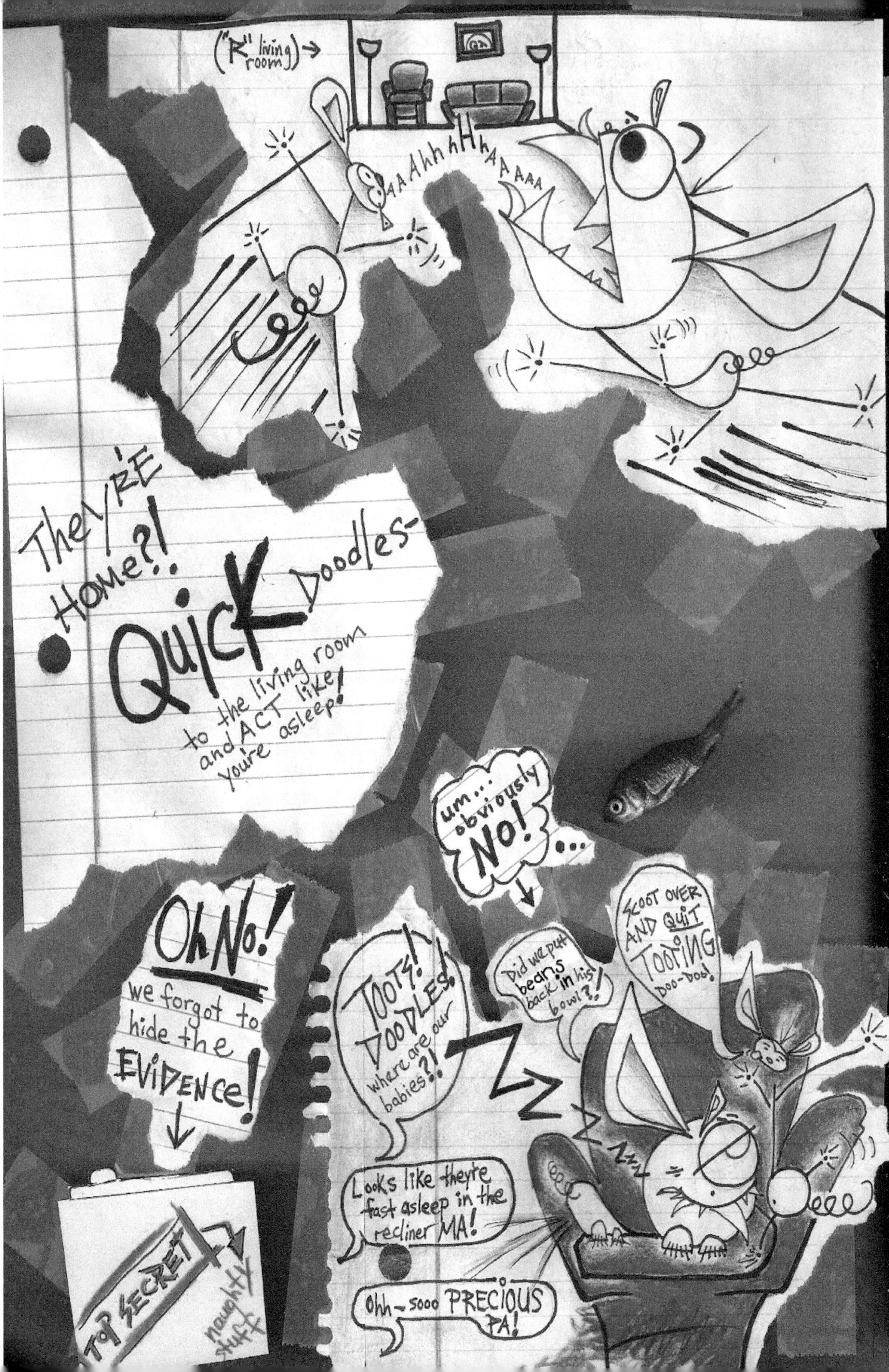

("R" living room) →
AAAhhhHhAAAAA
They'RE HOME?!
QUICK Doodles-
to the living room and ACT like you're asleep!
um... obviously NO!...
Oh No!
we forgot to hide the EVIDENCE!
TOP SECRET
naughty stuff
TOOTS! DOODLES! where are our babies?!
Did we put beans back in his bowl?!
SCOOT OVER AND QUIT TOOTING DOO-DOO!
Looks like theyre fast asleep in the recliner MA!
Ohh~sooo PRECIOUS PA!

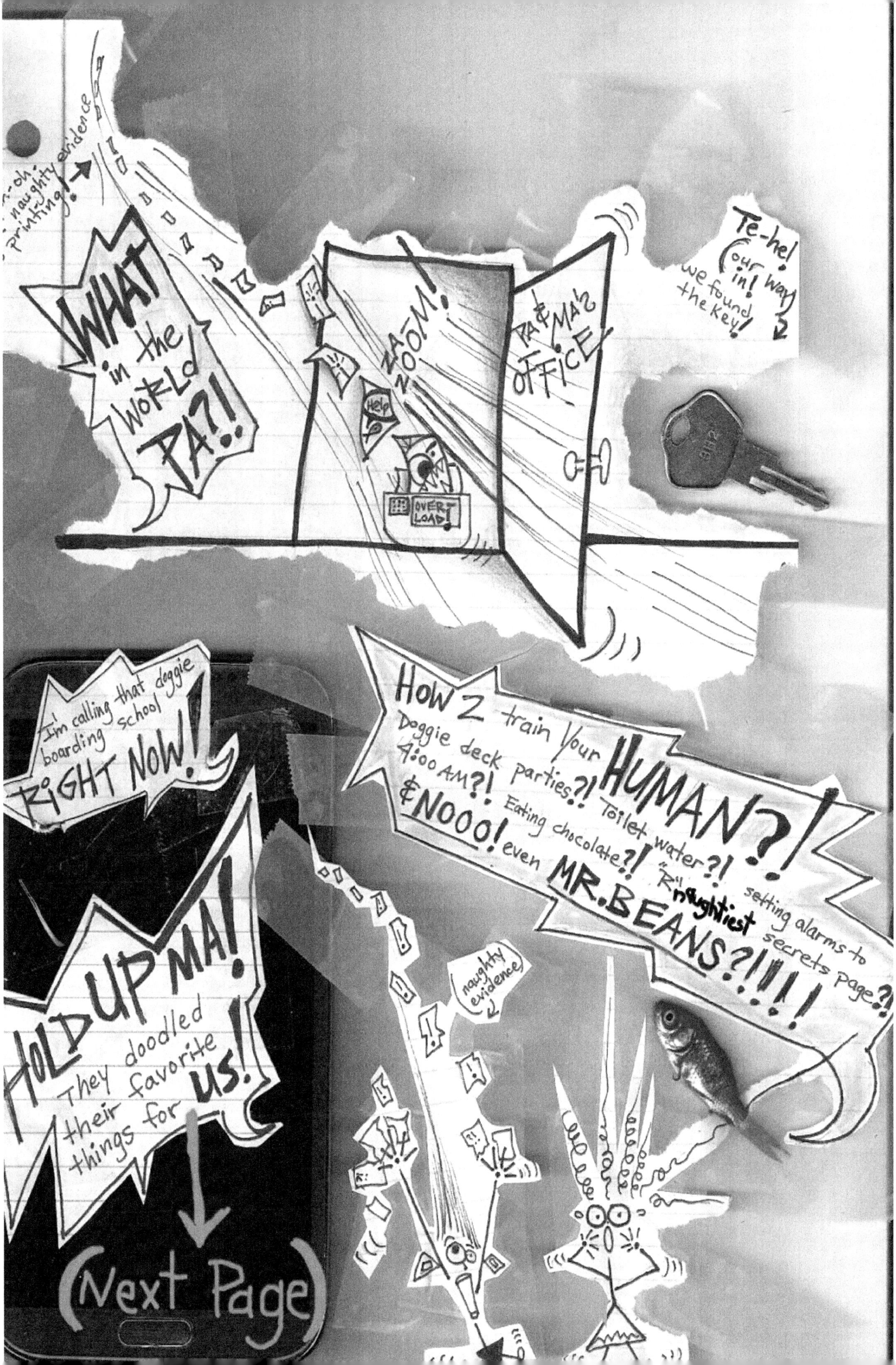
-oh. naughty evidence printing!
WHAT in the WORLD PA?!
ZOOM!
Help
OVERLOAD!
PA & MA's OFFICE
Te-he! (our way in!) we found the key!
I'm calling that doggie boarding school RIGHT NOW!
HOW 2 train your HUMAN?!
Doggie deck parties?! Toilet water?! setting alarms to 4:00 AM?! Eating chocolate?! "R" naughtiest secrets page?!
& NOOO! even MR. BEANS?!!!!!
HOLD UP MA! They doodled their favorite things for US!
(Next Page)
(naughty evidence)

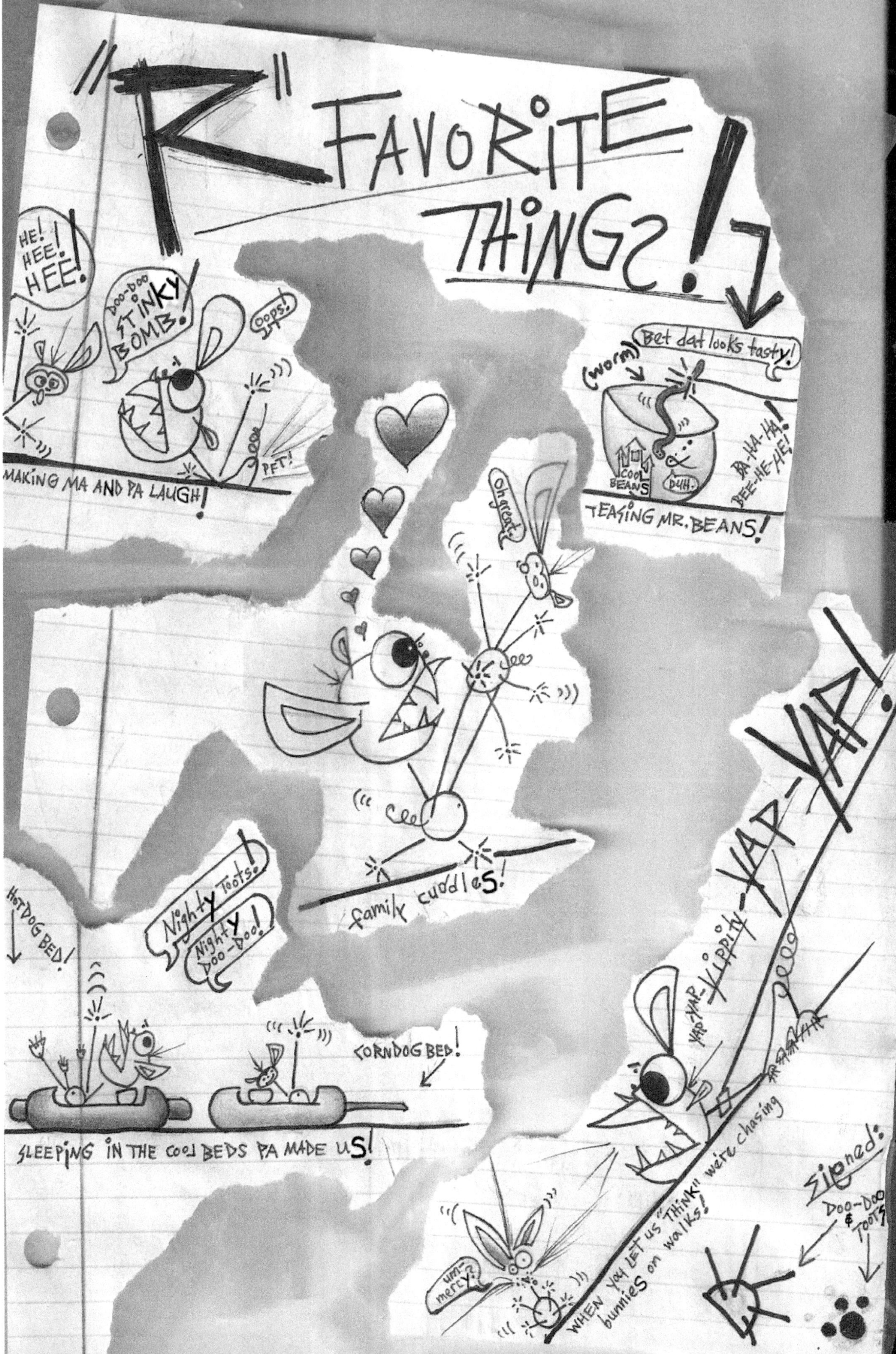
"R" FAVORITE THINGS!
HE! HEE! HEE!
DOO-DOO STINKY BOMB!
Oops!
PFT!
MAKING MA AND PA LAUGH!
Bet dat looks tasty!
(worm)
COOL BEANS
DUH.
BA-HA-HA! BEE-HE-HE!
TEASING MR. BEANS!
Oh great.
family cuddles!
Nighty Toots!
Nighty Doo-Doo!
HOTDOG BED!
CORNDOG BED!
SLEEPING IN THE COOL BEDS PA MADE US!
YAP-YAP-Kippity-YAP-YAP!
um-mercy?
WHEN you LET us "THINK" we're chasing bunnies on walks!
Signed:
Doo-Doo & Toots

"R" Favorite things!

(continued)

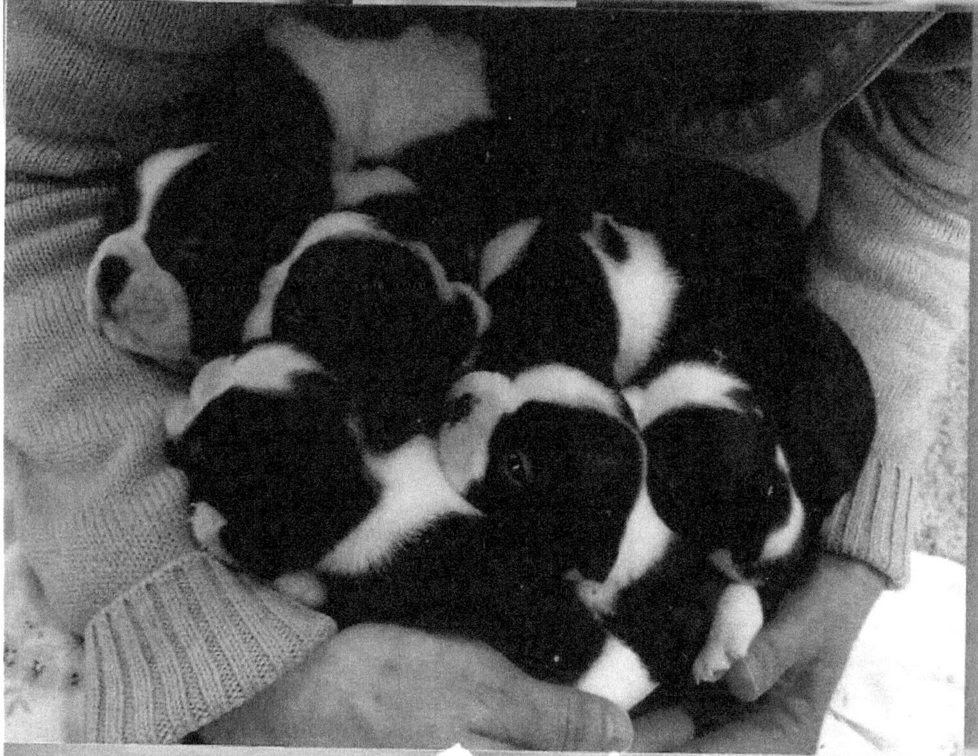

↑ Snuggles and Hugs!

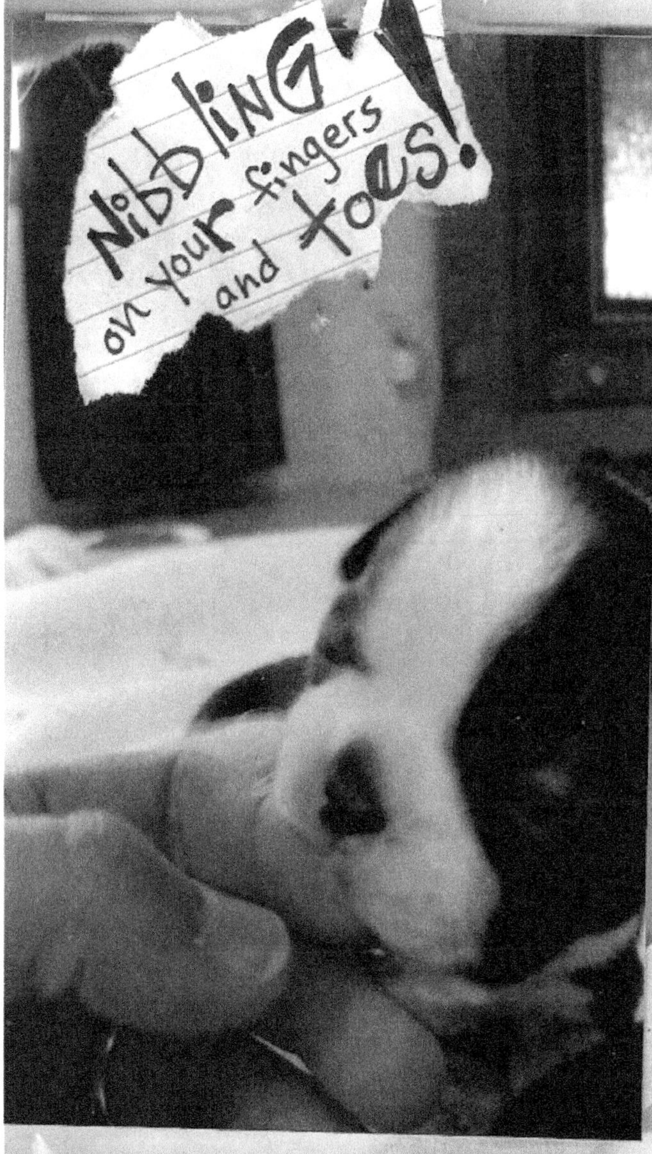

Nibbling on your fingers and toes!

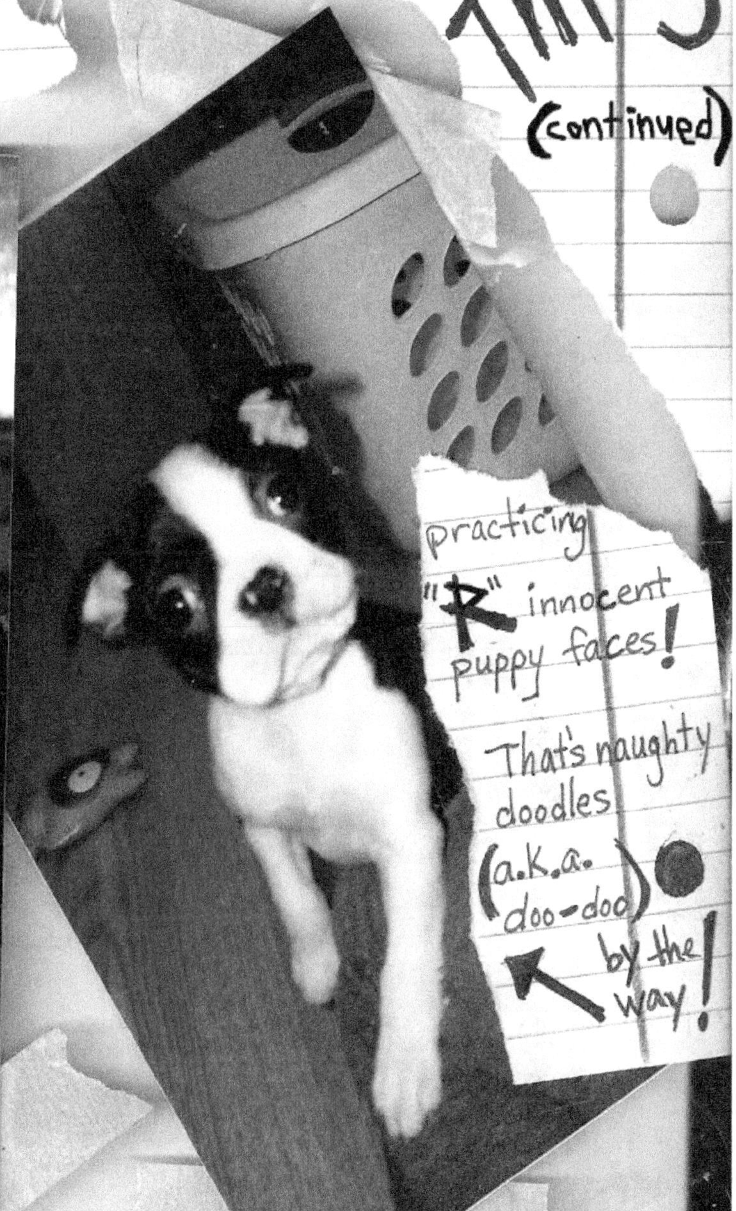

practicing "R" innocent puppy faces!

That's naughty doodles (a.k.a. doo-doo) ↖ by the way!

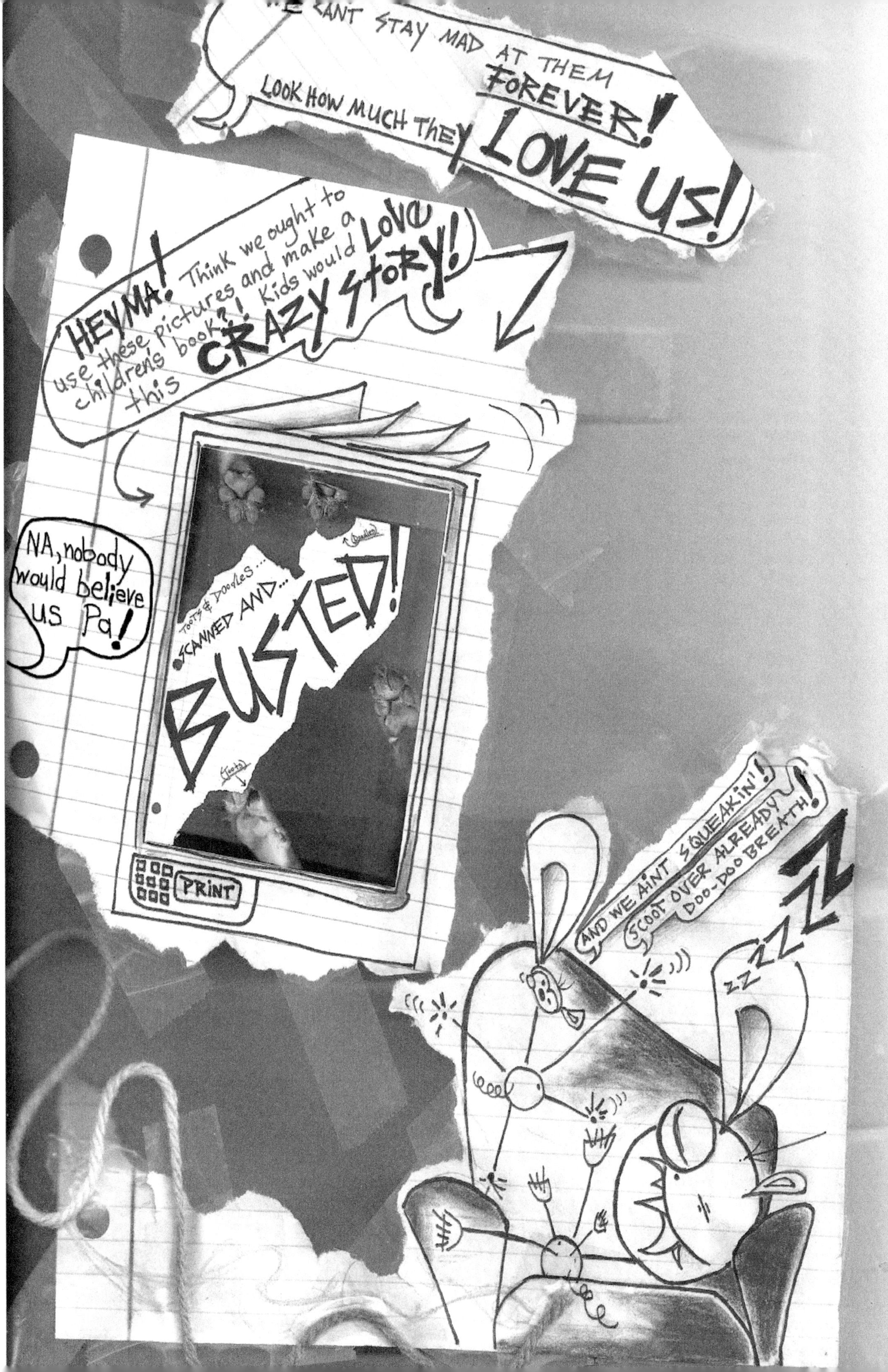

CANT STAY MAD AT THEM FOREVER!
LOOK HOW MUCH THEY LOVE US!
HEY MA! Think we ought to use these pictures and make a children's book?! Kids would LOVE this CRAZY STORY!
NA, nobody would believe us Pa!
(Doodles)
TOOTS & DOODLES ... SCANNED AND... BUSTED!
(Toots)
PRINT
AND WE AINT SQUEAKIN'!
SCOOT OVER ALREADY DOO-DOO BREATH!
zzzzZZ

About the Author/Illustrator

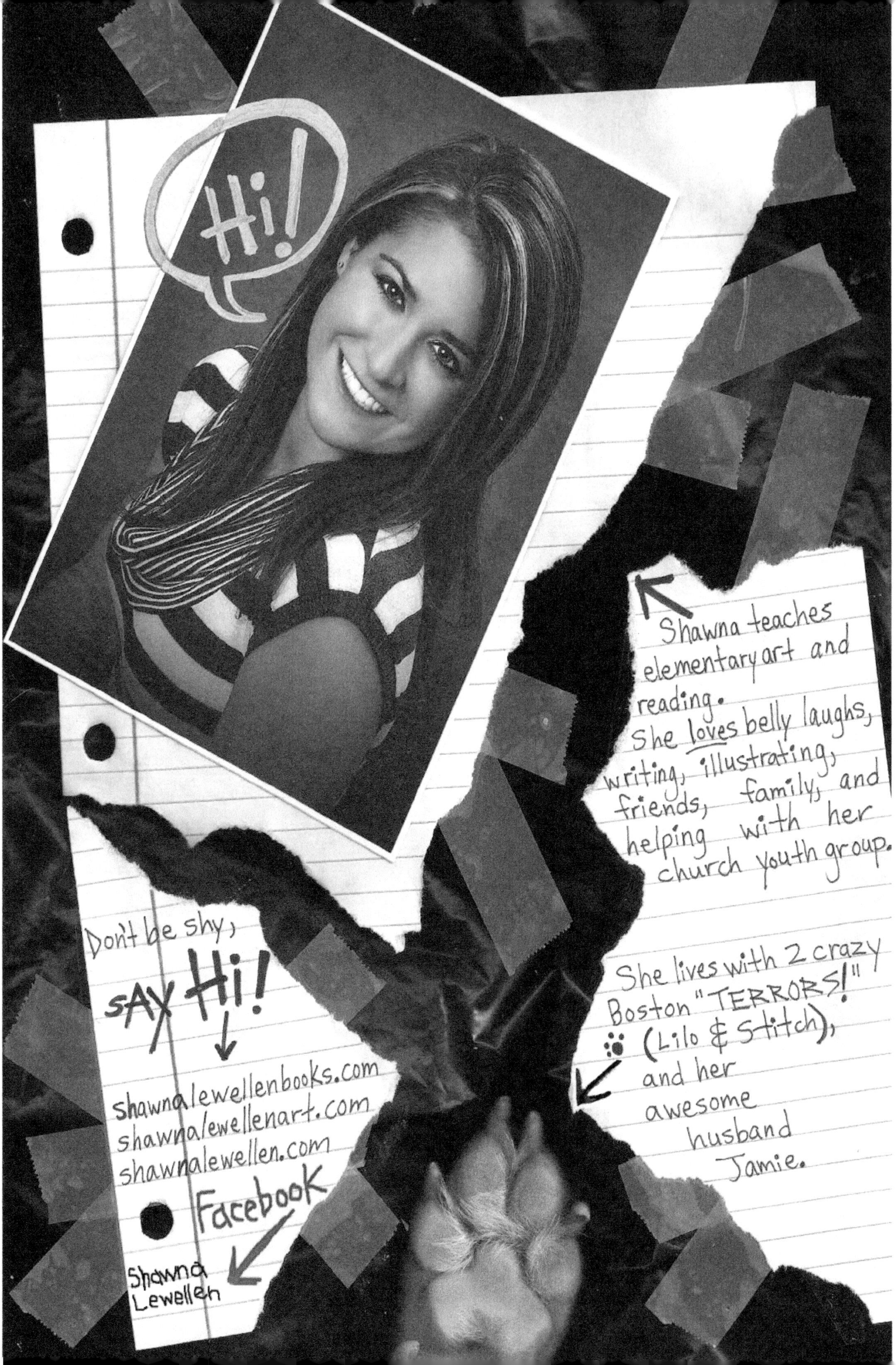
Hi!

Shawna teaches elementary art and reading.
She loves belly laughs, writing, illustrating, friends, family, and helping with her church youth group.

She lives with 2 crazy Boston "TERRORS!" (Lilo & Stitch), and her awesome husband Jamie.

Don't be shy,
SAY Hi!

shawnalewellenbooks.com
shawnalewellenart.com
shawnalewellen.com

Facebook
Shawna Lewellen

Shawna Lynn loves to connect with readers, and receiving emails, letters, drawings and photographs from kids.

Kids and parents, please free to contact Shawna Lynn at:
shawnalewellenbooks@gmail.com

To learn more about Shawna Lynn's upcoming books, please stop by her WEBSITE (http://shawnalewellenart.com/) and BLOG (http://shawnalewellen.com/)

Shawna invites you to stop by the Toots and Doodles website http://tootsanddoodles.com/

Follow Shawna Lynn on Facebook (https://www.facebook.com/shawna.m.lewellen?fref=ts)

CPSIA information can be obtained
at www.ICGtesting.com
Printed in the USA
LVOW05s0443210917
549464LV00014B/99/P